'Hey dude, this is *n*

Raphael suddenly st
wrong with the doc
usual. 'Hold it!' he

The Turtles dropped their carefree teen personas. Now they were four alert ninja with razor-keen fighting instincts. Their weapons were readied in an instant.

Taking a cautious step forward, Raphael eased open the door. They looked through, and their jaws dropped open in horror.

The den had been completely smashed up, apparently in a ferocious struggle. All their salvaged gear – the ghetto blaster, telephone booth and so on – lay in wrecked fragments around the floor.

There was no sign of their master.

Raphael rushed over to Splinter's empty chair. A dark streak stained the seat. He hardly dared to reach out his fingers and touch it. It was moist and red. Splinter's blood.

Raphael's forlorn howl of anguish ripped through the darkness of the sewers like a knife . . .

TEENAGE MUTANT NINJA TURTLES®

GOLDEN HARVEST PRESENTS A LIMELIGHT PRODUCTION IN ASSOCIATION WITH GARY PROPPER A STEVE BARRON FILM
TEENAGE MUTANT NINJA TURTLES® STARRING JUDITH HOAG ELIAS KOTEAS
BASED ON CHARACTERS CREATED BY KEVIN EASTMAN AND PETER LAIRD MUSIC BY JOHN DU PREZ
PRODUCTION DESIGNER ROY FORGE SMITH EXECUTIVE IN CHARGE OF PRODUCTION THOMAS K. GRAY EXECUTIVE PRODUCER RAYMOND CHOW CO-PRODUCER GRAHAM COTTLE STORY BY BOBBY HERBECK
SCREENPLAY BY TODD W. LANGEN AND BOBBY HERBECK PRODUCED BY KIM DAWSON, SIMON FIELDS, DAVID CHAN DIRECTED BY STEVE BARRON
Golden Harvest   DOLBY STEREO   ANIMATRONIC CHARACTERS BY JIM HENSON'S CREATURE SHOP

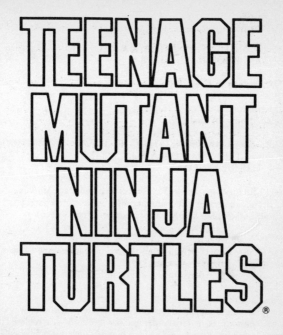

TEENAGE MUTANT NINJA TURTLES

A NOVELIZATION

Dave Morris

BANTAM BOOKS

TORONTO • NEW YORK • LONDON • SYDNEY • AUCKLAND

TEENAGE MUTANT NINJA TURTLES®
A BANTAM BOOK 0 553 40358 3

First publication in Great Britain

PRINTING HISTORY
Bantam edition published 1990

This book is set in 11/12 Sabon
by Falcon Typographic Art Ltd

Bantam Books are published by Transworld Publishers Ltd., 61-63
Uxbridge Road, Ealing, London W5 5SA, in Australia by Transworld
Publishers (Australia) Pty Ltd, 15-23 Helles Avenue, Moorebank,
NSW 2170, and in New Zealand by Transworld Publishers (NZ) Ltd,
Cnr Moselle and Waipareira Avenues, Henderson, Auckland.

Printed and bound in Great Britain by
Cox & Wyman Ltd, Reading, Berks.

1

New York was in the grip of a crime wave.

In itself this was nothing new. Violence and lawlessness has always festered under the murk of the metropolis. But now the style of crime was subtly different.

Instead of random muggings, there had been an increase in highly efficient robberies and burglaries. Watches and wallets would disappear while their owners were walking down a busy street. TVs and microwaves vanished from homes, but even if the owners were home they would report hearing nothing. Cars were spirited out of their parking spaces as if by magic.

It was obvious that there was an organized element behind the crimes. And whoever they were, they worked with the precision of craftsmen. There were no eyewitnesses to their crimes.

Even the victims themselves rarely knew they had been robbed until long after the event.

People called it 'The Silent Crime Wave'.

April O'Neil was angry about the rise in crime, and she was angry about the lack of any official response from City Hall. But you could hardly tell it from her TV report. On the Channel Three Eyewitness News, she came across as calm and incisive. April knew how to use her anger, how to direct it into a concise and biting summary of what was wrong – and what needed to be done about it.

April left the studio late, as usual. As one of Channel Three's top reporters, her career was important to her and she worked hard at it. Actually it was more than a career – almost a vocation. April saw herself as a spokesperson for all the little people of the city, the people whose grievances were too unimportant for those in authority to concern themselves about. She could give a voice to their hopes and fears. It pleased her that her report earlier that evening would have ruffled a few feathers down at City Hall.

Saying goodnight to the security guard, April pushed open the huge glass doors of the television studio. The parking lot was largely deserted at this hour – few of April's colleagues set themselves such an exhausting work schedule. She drew up the collar of her coat and set out with brisk paces towards where her van was parked, her heels beating out a gravelly staccato which echoed into the night.

As she passed a dumpster, a bottle fell to the ground only a few feet away. April whirled at the crash of breaking glass. Lost in thought as she was, the sudden noise had given her a fright. She was more frightened still by the sight of a rat scurrying away. April hated rats. With a cry of disgust she jumped up on to a crate.

The rat disappeared between a row of garbage cans lined up alongside the river that adjoined the parking lot. April watched it go with a shudder before climbing down from the crate. She was faintly ashamed at herself. She had covered some pretty hair-raising news stories in her time, all without batting an eyelid, but rats made her skin crawl. With a quicker step she continued on towards her van.

Out in the murky waters of the river, unnoticed by April, a large convex shape broke the surface and bobbed amid the floating debris. It looked like an overturned coracle. Another similar form surfaced, then another – and another. Moonlight glistened on the four shapes as they drifted along with the sluggish current.

April approached her vw van, already reaching into her bag for the keys. A row of remote broadcast trucks were parked off to one side. April turned towards them as the sound of smashing

9

glass startled her for the second time that night. But this time the cause was not a rat. Not the animal variety of rat, anyway. It was a gang of young street toughs stealing TV monitors from the trucks.

April felt pinned by the streetlight above her. She wanted to run, but her limbs seemed frozen. She had thought the rat had frightened her, but now she knew what real fear was.

A knife flashed in the lamplight. 'Bad timing,' rasped a voice.

April managed half a step backwards. 'You're telling me . . .' she managed to gulp.

Now that the initial shock had passed, April was thinking more clearly. She turned to make a run for it, but her heel twisted under her and she stumbled.

In moments the gang had surrounded her. Their grins were like wolf smiles, their knives like claws. The oldest one lunged forward and pinned her arms. April mustered a healthy scream which was stifled by a vicious backhand across her face. Before she could draw breath to cry out again, one of the thugs pressed a hand across her mouth.

April tried to twist away, to break the grip and lash out with a kick, but they were too many and too strong for her. One of them grabbed her hair and pulled her head back.

Her eyes were wide with panic. The streetlight blazed above her, blurred by tears of pain. She felt as though she was caught in an endless moment of terror. She heard the thugs muttering nastily to one another, but she picked up the sense of what they were going to do to her rather than taking in their words.

Oh, Mother of God, April pleaded inwardly. *Help me . . .*

Something sharp and silver flashed from out of the night. It shattered the streetlight, and the parking lot was plunged into darkness.

April heard something that sounded like a baseball bat whacking into a coconut. She did not realize what it was until she heard one of the thugs holding her give a stunned groan and then fall limply to the ground.

She took full advantage of this sudden godsend. Pulling away from her assailants, she pitched headlong on to the ground and began to scramble away. From behind her now came the sounds of a fast and very ferocious fistfight. A fistfight that – to judge by their whimpers and moans – the thugs who had attacked her were losing.

April's first instinct had been to get the hell out of there, but now that the immediate threat was gone her irrepressible reporter's curiosity took over. She scrambled only another few feet before she could no longer resist turning to watch.

There was not much to see. In the cloudy moonlight, and with tears of pain still filling her eyes, she could just make out vague shapes. They leapt and cartwheeled among the confused thugs like cannonballs, lashing out with punishing kicks and punches.

April realized that the sound of a police siren was approaching. Turning, she called out, 'Over here! Over here!', then looked back to discover that the fight was over. Mysterious footsteps retreated softly into the night. Only seconds later, two squad cars drew into the parking lot and screeched to a halt, their headlights illuminating an amazing scene . . .

The four thugs were squatting back-to-back on the ground, trussed together with a coil of coaxial cable. One of them had an aerial stuffed into the hood of his sweatshirt. With his two black eyes, it made him look like a dazed Martian.

The police officers rushed up and helped April to her feet. 'Hey,' said one, 'I seen you on the news?'

Still recovering from her narrow escape, April could only nod in reply.

'Mind telling us what happened here, miss?' put in one of the other officers.

April found her voice again. 'I – I wish I knew,' she gasped, running her hand through her hair. 'I must've taken a hefty knock on the head. I've been seeing things . . .'

She let the words trail off. She had no way to explain what she had seen to the policemen. She was not even sure herself. As the thugs were bundled off towards the squad car, though, April's gaze alighted on a metal object gleaming brightly in the headlights.

She stooped and picked it up. It was a strange kind of implement, with a long narrow central prong and two shorter ones on either side – like a cross between a dagger and a fork.

So this is what broke the streetlamp, thought April. She had a vague feeling she had seen something like it once before, but she could not remember if it was at a barbecue or in a martial arts movie.

The police were busy reading the thugs their rights. April quickly slipped the weapon into her bag.

Some distance away, unnoticed by either April or the police, a manhole cover slowly rose. A pair of masked eyes glared up, narrowing in annoyance as they watched April taking the weapon.

'Damn,' the unseen figure whispered to himself. He ducked down and silently lowered the manhole cover into place above him.

2

Deep in the sewers, a rat was gnawing on a piece of floating debris. The incessant drip-drip of slimy water echoed spectrally through the warren of tunnels and pipes. Then a chatter of voices could be heard, alarming the rat into abandoning its meal. It scuttled off into the shadows as three bulky shapes hove into view at the end of the tunnel.

The three shapes came loping along the tunnel. A human observer would have been dumbfounded at the sight. They walked on two legs and spoke like teenagers – but they looked like giant turtles! Or like some kind of hybrid between human and turtle. And they wore the masks and combat gear of ninja, the ancient Japanese warriors.

They were the Teenage Mutant Ninja Turtles.

Leonardo came first, his katana sword sheathed

across his back. 'We were awesome, bros! Awesome!' he called back over his shoulder.

Leonardo, as the eldest, was the group's unofficial leader. Once he had spoken, it gave the signal to the others that they were well away from prying eyes and ears. They could relax.

'Yes, ladies and gentlemen,' said Michaelangelo, twirling his deadly nunchaku sticks like a football rattle as he imitated a sportscaster, 'it looks like major league butt-kicking is back in town!'

The third Turtle was Donatello, the group's intellectual. He was more softly spoken and introspective than his brothers. Lifting his bo staff over his head, he gave a delighted laugh. '*Oh*, yeah.'

Leonardo was in a more overtly jubilant mood. Punching the air, he repeated. 'Awesome!'

Michaelangelo caught up and gave him a clap on the back of the shell. '*Right*eous!'

Donatello exuberantly joined in – or tried to. 'Bossa Nova!' he cried.

The other two paused and turned to look back at him.

'Uh . . . Chevy Nova?' ventured Donatello.

More looks. Donatello was not very good at this. He tried imitating Michaelangelo: '*Ex*-cellent!'

The others laughed and dragged him forward so that they were marching arm in arm like the Three Musketeers. 'Come on, guys, let's move it,' said Michaelangelo. 'I'm starvin' after that workout!'

There was a fourth Turtle, Raphael – 'Mr Intensity' his brothers called him when they were in an unkind mood. He followed more slowly, eyes deep in reflection under his red mask. As the Turtles reached the door of their secret hideaway, Raphael glared down at his belt. Where he should have had two sharp sai-daggers there was now only one.

Raphael took a last glance back down the tunnel. 'Damn,' he muttered again under his breath. Then he followed his brothers into the den.

For a sewer dwelling, the place was very warm and comfortable. It was furnished with various items that the Turtles had salvaged from the sewers and repaired. Some were quite astonishing. There was a sofa, a rusting but still functional telephone booth, and an old television. Donatello had even rigged up electric lights and had converted the exposed steam pipes into a form of central heating.

'Master,' said Leonardo, bowing as he entered. His tone was one of reverence now, a marked contrast to his jollity before. Struggling to control his excitement, he rushed forward and knelt before his ninja master. 'We have had our first battle, Master Splinter,' he went on. 'They were many, but we kicked their . . . I mean, we fought well.'

Splinter nodded slowly. He too was a mutant – but no turtle. He resembled a rat about four feet tall, his fur greying with age, and with a chunk missing from his right ear. He wore a patched-up kimono and tabi shoes. The most remarkable thing about him was his aura of calm wisdom

– the legacy of years of meditation and ninjutsu training. His eyes were sharp but serene.

When he spoke, his voice was a balm of tranquillity. 'Were you seen?'

Leonardo shook his head.

Splinter gave a single nod, a gesture of satisfaction at his pupils' performance. 'In this you must never lapse. Even those who might be our allies would not understand. You must strike hard, then fade away without a trace. This is the way of ninjutsu.'

Donatello flashed the slightest of glances at Raphael. It was all the indication that Splinter needed to realize something was amiss. He looked at Raphael and waited for him to speak.

Raphael was angry at himself, and disappointed by his mistake. Under his master's gentle probing gaze, he blurted out what had happened. 'I lost a sai.'

'Then it is gone,' Splinter said calmly.

Raphael was ashamed, and anxious to make amends. He had no plan in mind, but he said, 'I can get it back, *sensei*. I can . . .'

'Raphael. Let it go.' Splinter turned to address them all. 'Your ninja skills are reaching their peak. Only one truly important lesson remains, but must wait. I know it is hard for you here, underground; your teenage minds are broad, eager. But you must never stop practising the techniques of ninjutsu – the art of invisibility . . .'

Splinter became aware that one of his pupils

was not listening. Michaelangelo had sidled over to the phone and was ordering dinner – the Turtles' favourite food, pizza. As he specified the toppings, Splinter called him to order with a brusque, 'Michaelangelo!'

Mike gave his master a weak smile and quickly finished: '. . . An' the clock's tickin', dude!' He hung up and bowed in apology.

Splinter waited until all four of his pupils were listening. 'You are still young,' he continued, 'but I am old. One day I will be gone. You must be ready to fend for yourselves when that day comes. Use my teachings wisely.' He paused. 'Now, I suggest we all meditate on the events of this evening.'

Splinter closed his eyes and began the breathing exercises of Zen meditation. But only a few seconds had gone by before he was startled out of his tranquillity by the blaring of party music. He snapped his eyes open to see Michaelangelo and Donatello dancing beside their ghetto blaster, jerking frenetically to the beat of *Tequila*. As the break in the cadence came, the two brothers stopped, pointed to each other, and in their deepest voices intoned, 'Nin*ju*tsu!' before picking up again.

As Donatello spun on his shell in the Turtles' unique form of breakdancing, Michaelangelo finally noticed his master's disapproving look. 'Uh, well, this is like meditating . . .' he ventured. 'A bit.'

Splinter sighed and gave a slight roll of his eyes before closing them again. But there was the hint of a smile on his bewhiskered face. He knew that his pupils were young, and they needed some moments of relaxation in the midst of their strenuous training. Tonight they had earned their fun. Let them celebrate their victory – later they could meditate.

Leonardo, the most dedicated of the four, had settled down beside his master. Even he could not resist swaying along to the music with his upper body however. When he saw that Splinter was content to let the others enjoy themselves, he started to get up to join them. Then he noticed that Raphael was putting on a trenchcoat and fedora. It was the Turtles' standard disguise when they wanted to walk about the city streets unnoticed.

'Hey, Raph,' he said. 'Where ya goin'?'

Raphael was still peeved. He was in no mood for the usual kidding around with his brothers. At times like this he preferred some time on his own. That was his form of meditation. 'Out to a movie,' he snapped back. 'That OK with you?'

Leonardo shrugged as if to say, 'Sorry I asked.' He was about to add that he would miss the pizza in that case, but the door of the den swung shut. Raphael was already gone.

3

Elsewhere in the city, there was a young man who could match the intensity of Raphael's anger.

Casey Jones was watching TV. He did this every night, flicking randomly between channels, even though it only seemed to make him angrier. The news report was about the mysterious crime wave, focusing tonight on the rise in personal assaults. Police spokesmen, as usual, could throw no light on the matter.

Casey tried another channel. It was a movie showing a woman screaming in terror. A third channel was running a cop show – Casey saw three men fall in a blaze of gunfire and wailing sirens, all in the space of seconds. Yet another channel was running a documentary about terrorists in the Middle East. They had bombed a bus and killed a dozen schoolkids.

Casey's pulse was pounding in his temples. He was in his mid-twenties, with long dishevelled black hair. The beat-up old armchair and the television were about his only furniture. Apart from that, the apartment was filled with bits of sports equipment – baseball bats, pads, dumb-bells, footballs. The walls were plastered with sports posters; mostly they were of violent sports like boxing or full-contact karate. In one corner was a bare mattress with a stack of grubby comic books beside it. The place looked a lot less homely than the Turtles' sewer den.

Casey did not care. He hardly noticed his sur-roundings anyway. All of his attention was concen-trated obsessively on the television, and all he saw there were pictures of escalating violence. Casey thought that the rest of the world was going mad.

For someone who claimed to detest violence, Casey Jones was strangely allured by it. Eyes widened in an intense stare, he seemed almost hypnotized by the images as he flipped from chan-nel to channel. A scene of slaughter in Bolivia – a gangster gunning down his rivals – film of a plane crash – a spy series with a bloody fistfight —

Click. Casey sat in darkness and silence, drawing his breath raggedly through flared nostrils. Some-thing had to be done. Someone had to stop this terrible tide of violence.

He picked up a hockey mask and slipped it over his face. It took away the vulnerable humanity, left only the intense stare of his angry eyes. It made

Casey feel like an implacable avenger. He was a masked vigilante of the night. A lone warrior for justice. Just like . . .

Behind the mask, Casey grinned and hefted a bat.

Down in the sewer outside the Turtles' den, Donatello was doing some lazy s-curves on his skateboard along the tunnel wall. Michaelangelo slouched nearby beneath a grating, his arms folded in impatience.

Donatello ambled over and stared up through the grating. The moon was just emerging from behind a rack of cloud – a disc of silver in a field of velvet blue-black. Donatello drew his breath in a sigh. His sense of wonder never left him, and he always found himself marvelling at the myriad beauties of the upper world. If only he and his brothers could walk around freely up there . . .

He glanced at Michaelangelo. The moonlight passing through the grille cast a pattern of shadows like prison bars. 'Nice night, Mike.'

Michaelangelo glanced up and gave a noncommittal grunt. He was less interested in the night sky than in his stomach. 'Pizza dude's got thirty seconds,' he grumbled, pointing at his watch.

Donatello dropped to a crouch beside his brother. 'Hey, Mike . . .' he began hesitantly. 'You ever think about what Master Splinter said tonight? I mean about what it would be like . . . you know, without him?'

Michaelangelo did not answer immediately. He disliked thinking about things that upset him. He preferred every moment of life to be fun. He could leave the serious stuff to the others. And he certainly did not want to think about life without the guiding hand of his beloved mentor.

Instead, he changed the subject. 'Time's up! That's three bucks off.'

Donatello understood. Sometimes he even envied Michaelangelo his carefree attitude, though he thought it was always better to talk things through than to hide them away inside you. He touched his brother on the arm, then hopped on to the skateboard and took off down the tunnel towards the den.

Shoes scuffed the pavement above the grating, and Michaelangelo glanced up. Someone was muttering to himself in frustration. Michaelangelo hauled himself up for a closer look.

It was the pizza delivery man. He had a pizza box in his hand and was staring at the address slip on it. 'Oh, swell!' he grumbled in a thick Brooklyn accent. 'Terrific! An' where da heck is one-twenty-two an' an *eighth* —?'

'You're standing on it, dude!' announced Michaelangelo.

The delivery man jumped like a startled cat. It was a couple of seconds before he could pluck up the nerve to step back closer to the grate, where he could now see the tip of a bill waving enticingly. 'What da . . .?'

'Just slip the pizza down here,' came Michaelangelo's voice from the sewer.

The delivery man took a couple of steps closer, holding out the pizza box tentatively in front of him until it touched the grate. He had made deliveries to some real weirdos in the past, but this took the cake. Or rather, the pizza. As he felt the box tugged out of his hand, he snatched the bill and backpedalled to a safe distance.

But when he looked at the bill more closely in the light of the streetlamp, all trepidation vanished to be replaced by a lusty measure of Brooklyn indignation. 'Hey!' he yelled. 'Dis is only a ten! The tab's thirteen!'

Michaelangelo was beginning to duck back down into the tunnel. He glanced back and said, 'You're two minutes late, dude.'

The delivery man switched to a politer tone. 'Yeah, you're right – but come on, cut me a break here, will ya?'

Michaelangelo adopted a Confucius-he-say accent: 'Forgiveness is divine. But never pay full price for late pizza.' And with a laugh, he vanished off into the tunnels.

'OK, guys,' Michaelangelo announced as he flung open the door of the den. 'It's pizza time!'

As the others gathered around the table, Michaelangelo borrowed one of Leonardo's katana for his favourite party trick. Impersonating the announcer on a TV ad, he tossed the pizza up into the air and said, 'Yes, friends, the new "Turbo Ginsu" . . .'

The katana blade swished through the air.

'. . . It slices, it dices – and, yes, makes french fries *three* different ways.'

Neatly sliced in midair, the sections of pizza fell on to plates in front of each Turtle. Unfortunately, Michaelangelo had not allowed for his master's long snout – Splinter's pizza slice dropped splat on top of his head.

'Uh, well, maybe it needs some practice . . .' ventured Michaelangelo, trying to suppress a smile as Splinter glared at him from under a wedge of tomato sauce and melted cheese.

4

The movie Raphael had gone to see was *Critters*. It had done little to lighten his mood. As he left the cinema with the rest of the crowd, he pulled his collar up and hat down to conceal his reptilian features.

'*Critters*!' he muttered to himself. 'Where do they come *up* with this stuff?' Raphael preferred a bit of realism in a movie. He wished he had gone to see *Ninja Wars* instead.

As he walked back towards the storm drain cover that led home to the sewers, Raphael heard a cry of alarm. Disinterestedly turning his head, he saw two teenaged hoodlums robbing an old lady. One had distracted her by asking for the time while the other snatched her purse. One thing was for sure – they weren't part of 'The Silent Crime Wave'. They were much too amateurish for that.

Raphael stuck out his foot to trip the one with the purse. As the youth went sprawling, Raphael yanked the purse out of his hand and tossed it back to the old lady in one fluid motion. Then he stuck his hand back into the pocket of his trenchcoat before anyone noticed it was green – and had only three fingers.

Raphael did not wait around to be thanked. Pressing through the crowd of onlookers, he made his way over to the entrance to Central Park. He did not much like having to draw attention to himself – it went against the grain of everything Splinter had taught him. The park would be pretty much deserted, though. He decided on a short walk before heading home.

The two young muggers had darted away as soon as their mugging was foiled. They, too, had chosen the darkened park as a place to lie low for a few minutes and get their breath back.

'Did you get a look at that guy who tripped me?' panted the purse-snatcher.

'Yeah,' said the other. 'Was that a halloween mask or what?'

'I hate those have-a-go heroes,' spat the first, recovering a measure of bravado along with his breath. 'They make the mugging business a real pain.'

There was a crash in the bushes as someone dropped from an overhanging tree branch to land behind them. The two hoodlums whirled, frozen in shock at the sight of a burly figure in a hockey

mask. His cut-off sweatshirt revealed rippling muscles, and he had a golf bag on his back filled with
various clubs, bats and sticks. The hoodlums had
no idea who he was, but it was obvious he had not
dropped in to sell them life insurance.

'You call that a pain?' growled Casey. 'You
purse-grabbing pukes – *this* is pain!'

Drawing a hockey stick from his bag, Casey
lashed out viciously. One of the hoodlums shrieked
as the stick laid open a nasty gash over his eyes. As
he staggered back, whimpering, Casey tore into the
other one.

'The penalty is two minutes for slashing . . .'
chortled Casey, enjoying himself more than he had
in years. He whacked the hoodlum in the stomach.
'. . . Two minutes for hooking . . .' The stick swung
round to hit the hoodlum across the knees, bowling him over. Casey raised it over his head, ready
to bring it down in a crunching blow on to his
moaning victim. 'And let's not forget my personal
favourite: two minutes for high sticking!'

Before the stick could descend, a trenchcoated
figure came flying out of the shadows and pounded
Casey in the small of the back. He went sprawling across his intended victim, more surprised
than hurt.

Raphael stood over him, his fists clenched. His
voice was full of righteous anger as he snarled,
'How 'bout a five minute "game misconduct" for
roughing, pal?' Raphael had no time for purse-
snatchers either, but he knew there was a world of

29

difference between foiling a robbery and beating two teenagers to a pulp with a hockey stick.

Casey scrambled to his feet, doing a doubletake as he got a better look at his assailant. In the gloom, he still could not make out the features under the hat and coat. 'Who're you, Humphrey Bogart?' he jibed. 'I got news for you, "pal" – you ain't the referee in this match. You did your bit, now get outta here and let me do mine. These juvenile low-lifes need a lesson.'

Raphael's anger became cold and stern. 'Not like that, they don't. Not from you.'

The hoodlums, in the meantime, had taken the opportunity to inch back away from the smouldering standoff. Now, with a glance at one another, they broke and ran.

Casey seethed with rage as he saw his prey getting away. It looked like he was going to miss out on his fun – but in that case he would just have to take out his disappointment on this stranger in the trenchcoat. He reached into his bag and pulled out two baseball bats. 'Looks like you're the one who needs the lesson,' he said to Raphael. 'The class is Pain 101. Your instructor: Casey Jones . . .'

Raphael's martial arts training had always taught him to use violence only to neutralize another's violence. He disapproved of this vicious madman in the hockey mask, but he had no particular desire to hurt him. 'Look,' he said. 'I don't wanna fight you . . .'

Casey ignored him. 'Tough rocks, "pal".'

With that, he leapt forward to the fray, swinging his two bats like scythes.

Raphael jumped and ducked the attacks with ease. 'Baseball, huh?' he quipped. 'Now, that's *my* kinda game.'

Casey was powerful and full of fighting spirit, but he could not hope to match Raphael's skill. The Turtle put up a hand and effortlessly stopped one of the bats, ducking under the other as he read the label.

'A "Wade Boggs" bat, eh?' he sneered. 'Tell me you didn't pay *money* for this.'

Casey could see that Raphael was just playing with him, and he hated to be mocked. Enraged, he lashed out with the other bat and landed a blow which knocked his opponent down.

'It was a two-for-one sale,' he said, smiling in satisfaction behind the mask. Then he looked closer, and leaned forward to stare. Raphael's hat had been dislodged during their battle, and Casey could make out some very odd features in the dim light. 'Hey, what *are* you?' he continued. 'Some sort of punker? I hate punkers. Especially bald ones in green makeup. Who wear masks. Over ugly faces . . .'

Taunts stung Raphael just as much as they did Casey. He was really steaming with anger as he got to his feet. Grabbing the bat he had been holding on to when he was knocked down, he advanced on Casey. 'New batter,' he said.

Raphael took a swing, but Casey dodged back. 'Strike one!' he announced.

Another swing, also a miss. 'Strike two! Three strikes an' you're *out*, punker.'

Fairly boiling with rage, Raphael moved in and executed a perfect forward flip high into the air over Casey's head. Before the vigilante could see where he had gone, he swung the bat around and struck him from behind. Casey gave a grunt and pitched headlong to the ground.

'Home run,' declared the triumphant Turtle, planting his foot in the middle of Casey's back. 'Raph wins with a score of one-nothing.'

Casey recovered fast. Rolling out from under Raphael's foot, he sprang to his feet and pulled a different kind of bat out of the bag. 'New game, roundhead,' he said. 'Cricket.'

'*Cricket?*' Raphael shook his head in disbelief. '*Nobody* understands cricket. You gotta know what a silly midoff is to follow cricket.'

Casey shrugged. 'It's easy. I'll teach you . . .'

Powerful muscles propelled the cricket bat in a wide arc. It caught Raphael at an unexpected angle before he could dodge. Arms flailing, he stumbled back into a wire mesh trash can.

'Ya see?' said Casey. 'That's six runs.'

Raphael struggled to free himself, but he was caught in the bin. As he fumed, Casey gave a final snort of derision and then ran off. But Raphael was not finished yet. Bending the wire mesh with his strong fingers, he raced in pursuit. He was really mad now, and he was damned if he was going to let some muscle-bound vigilante get away with making a fool of him.

Casey tore across the street and ducked into an alleyway. Raphael was hot on his heels. He saw Casey disappear through a cloud of steam pouring up through a drain and without thinking, ran straight after him.

It was a mistake. Casey had immediately reversed direction, and as Raphael came through the steam cloud he greeted him with a fist to the face. It was in fact a tactic worthy of a ninja, and Raphael might have granted Casey a certain rueful admiration if he had not just been laid flat out on his back.

Casey waved his hands as though shushing imagined applause. 'I know how you punkers enjoy pain. No need to thank me.'

Raphael suddenly swept Casey's feet out from under him, deftly swinging on top and applying an unbreakable stranglehold. '*Now* who's the champ, pal?' he hissed into Casey's ear. 'Who is? Huh?'

Casey was choking. 'OK, you're the champ . . .' he managed to gasp; for his self-esteem, he could not resist adding, '. . . ya freak.'

This jibe was the last straw for the angry Turtle. His blood was boiling. Tightening his grip, he snarled. 'The name's not "freak". It's Raphael. Can you say "Raphael"?'

Casey's eyes were almost popping out of his head. Raphael seemed oblivious of the fact that he was on the verge of killing him. With the very last of his air, he weakly gasped, '. . . Raphael.'

Raphael released his grip. 'I knew you could do it,' he said as he got up off Casey.

Weakened and half-fainting, Casey staggered to his feet. 'Man . . . you're *crazy*,' he gasped.

Raphael stared at him. '*I'm* crazy?'

Casey began to hasten away. 'You might've killed me! You're crazy. And dangerous.'

Raphael was flabbergasted. 'Dangerous!? *I'm* dangerous? You're the whacko with the bag of sticks, pal!'

Casey vanished off into the darkness, leaving the confused Turtle to ponder the implication of what had happened. He had intervened with the best of intentions when Casey had attacked the teenagers in the park, but then he had allowed it to become a grudge fight. Splinter had taught the Turtles their ninja skills to fight for justice, but Raphael knew he could have seriously injured a man tonight. Maybe Casey was right – maybe he might even have killed him. Despite all his training, his anger had got the better of him.

He picked up a trash can and, with a howl of frustration, hurled it away down the alley.

5

Raphael returned home to the sewers late. He had had some thinking to do. Really, it wasn't thinking. It was more like brooding.

He quietly eased the door open and entered the darkened lair. His brothers were asleep, snoring. Raphael pushed the door shut very slowly. It emitted the faintest of creaks, but the snoring continued.

As he turned to go to his room, a match flared to life. Splinter's face was illuminated in the glow, his limpid black eyes wide open and drinking in the light. Raphael, caught in the act of tiptoeing across the room, stopped dead in his tracks.

'Raphael,' said Splinter softly. 'Come sit by me.'

Raphael glanced at the door to his room. He was in no mood for one of his master's pep talks right now. He would sooner get some sleep.

'Could this wait till morning, *sensei*?' he asked.

Splinter watched him, unblinking. 'You will listen *now*,' he ordered.

Raphael moved over obediently and sat at Splinter's feet. The aged rat lit a candle and then turned back to his pupil.

'My ninjutsu master's name was Yoshi,' he told the Turtle. 'His first rule was, "Possess the right thinking. Only then can one receive the gifts of strength, knowledge and peace".'

Raphael sat quietly, trying to look attentive. Splinter's chest heaved in a deep sigh. 'I have tried to channel your anger, Raphael,' he continued, 'but more remains. Anger clouds the mind. Turned inward, it is an unconquerable enemy. You are unique among your brothers, for you choose to face this enemy alone. But as you face it, do not forget them. And do not forget me . . .'

Splinter gently reached out and laid his hand on Raphael's head. 'I am here, my son,' he concluded quietly.

Raphael rose and bowed, then moved off to his room. He moved as quickly as ninjutsu etiquette would allow.

He didn't want his master to see the tears in his eyes.

Early the next morning, there was a ring at April O'Neil's door. She opened the door to find her boss, Charles Pennington, and his thirteen-year-old son Danny. Charles had an expression of studied concern on his face. Danny wore his usual sullen frown and, for some reason, had a pair of stereo headphones resting on his neck.

'Charles,' she said. 'I'm just getting ready for work.'

Pennington came in and steered Danny over to the sofa as April vanished into the bathroom. Pennington went over and called through the door, having to raise his voice over the sound of splashing water.

'You could have called me last night, April,' he said. 'Call it a quirk, but I like to know when one of my top reporters has been mugged.'

April turned off the taps for a moment. 'It wasn't a mugging, Charles,' she called out. 'Besides, I knew you'd just get into a flap and rush over here. As you have.'

Charles was adamant. 'From now on, Security's escorting you out to that Stone Age van of yours at night.' It was an order.

April came to the bathroom door and gave him a mock salute. 'Yes, *sir*.'

Danny was sitting on the sofa reading a comic book. He had no interest in what his father and April were talking about. So what if she'd nearly been mugged? That kind of thing happened all the time in New York, didn't it? Finishing the comic book, he glanced around. April's purse rested on the coffee table beside him. He put his hand in, pulled out some cash and stuffed it into the pocket of his jeans. After a quick look round to check that his father hadn't noticed, he picked up another comic book.

Charles was standing looking out of the window. Below in the streets, people were already milling about like ants, so eager to get to work that they had no time for each other. He gave a philosophical sigh.

'Just what's going on out there, April?' he said. 'It's getting so you can't even step outside in the daytime any more.'

At least this was a subject that interested April. She walked through, putting on her earrings. 'I'll tell you this,' she said. 'After all the stuff I've been hearing out of Little Tokyo, Chief Sterns is going to have some answering to do when I interview him at City Hall this afternoon.'

Charles gave a groan. He knew what April could be like in an interview when she had an axe to grind. 'Just take it easy, will you, April?' he said — without any real hope that she would. 'Sterns has already got the Mayor breathing down my neck.'

April knew better than to rise to the bait. She had no intention of compromising her duty as a reporter just because of a little behind-the-scenes network politics.

Rather than argue, she turned to Danny and changed the subject: 'How's school going?'

Danny opened his mouth to answer, but Pennington did it for him — much to his son's chagrin. 'Oh, just *wonderful*,' he said in a disgusted tone. 'So wonderful, in fact, that I have to drive him there every morning now just to make sure he goes.'

Danny gave his father a resentful look and, tight-lipped, placed the headphones over his ears. Sullenly he turned his attention back to the comic book.

Pennington gave a resigned sigh. 'That's what he does when he wants to ignore me — sticks those things on.' He half turned to April, then glanced back. 'I'd like to know where he *got* them, too . . .'

6

Despite a layer of makeup powder, Police Chief Sterns was sweating like a pig. He found the TV lights too hot, and being interviewed live always made him nervous. All the reporters were clever-clever graduates like this April O'Neil – full of smart questions that could make him look stupid. What did any of *them* know about how to run a police department? Sterns resented having to talk to the press at all. After all, what did the viewing public know – or care – about the measures that had to be taken? They demanded instant results, but things just were not that simple. And when things went wrong – like now, with the so-called 'silent' crime wave – who was it who got the blame? Him, Chief Sterns.

Sterns looked at April and tried not to scowl. He twisted his fingers together hard and tried not to seem rattled by her questions. Taking a deep breath, he said, 'We do most definitely have active measures under way. Presently we're executing a plan of redeployment that will minimize response time by maximizing coordination between patrol units in a decentralized networking scheme.'

Sterns rocked back on his heels and allowed himself a self-satisfied smirk. Surely *that* had told her. That would impress the punters and the couch potatoes.

April allowed a moment to pass. 'I'm not sure I followed all that, Chief Sterns,' she said, holding out her microphone. 'Would you mind repeating it? In English, perhaps?'

Sterns addressed her as one might a notably stupid child. 'It means, Miss O'Neil, that we have everything well in hand.'

'Ah,' said April. 'Then you know who's behind these crimes?'

'Well, no . . . I didn't say that . . .' Sterns stuffed a stubby finger down his collar. This suddenly wasn't going well.

'But you know why the crimes have been escalating recently?' persisted April.

'No, I didn't say that *either*, Miss O'Neil. Maybe if you'd stick to asking *questions* there'd be less confusion.' There, that had told her.

April gave a sweet smile. 'Fine, Chief . . . What do you know about an organization called The Foot Clan?'

Sterns stiffened, suddenly squirming. 'There is . . . no evidence, er, to link such a name to these incidents,' he blustered.

In a warehouse far off across town, an interested party was watching Sterns' unedifying performance on a bank of TV monitors. He was not impressed with Sterns, and he was annoyed by this reporter, April O'Neil. She was like a wasp – buzzing around, pricking with her insolent questions. Prying . . .

'Then you are denying that an organization called The Foot Clan exists?' April was saying.

The mysterious figure folded his arms. His movements were grand – stately and measured, like one accustomed to command. But he was also capable of sudden action. Drawing a slender shuriken from his sleeve, he flicked it at April's on-screen image. Though he seemed to employ the smallest of effort, the blade shot through the air like a bullet and struck one of the multiple screens. It lodged right between April's eyes.

The man snapped his fingers, and another silhouetted figure approached him from out of the recesses of the warehouse. This second man was big and bald, with features like a bulldog. Without turning, the first man pointed at April's image and gave a terse command in Japanese.

The second figure bowed to his master. '*Hai!*' he said. It would be done.

Over in their den, the Turtles were also watching April's broadcast. Unlike the mysterious figure in the warehouse, they had nothing but praise for the tough line of questioning.

'Hey, that's the lady we saved!' said Donatello.

'An' she's really giving that shifty police chief a hard time,' said Leonardo admiringly. 'That's my kind of gal!'

Michaelangelo was star struck. 'I'm in *luv*,' he pantomimed, hand pressed to his heart.

Raphael rushed over to the TV set just as Sterns was winding up the interview. 'I'm not denying anything, Miss O'Neil,' the irascible police chief was saying. 'You're just putting words in my mouth as usual. Now, if you'll excuse me, I have more important matters to deal with.'

As Sterns retreated to his office, April turned to face the camera. 'We can only hope that one of them has something to do with solving these crimes,' she told the viewers. 'Live from City Hall, this is April O'Neil.'

April O'Neil . . . That was enough for Raphael. Now he had a name to go on, he could retrieve his lost sai and redeem the disgrace of his earlier slip-up in leaving it behind. Grabbing his disguise, he headed for the door.

Back at City Hall, Chief Sterns was not yet finished with April. As she and the film crew packed up their equipment, his voice blared out like a foghorn across the hallway: 'O'Neil!'

April handed her earpiece to a technician and grinned. 'Time me,' she said.

She crossed over and went into Chief Sterns' office. What she did not see was Danny Pennington being brought in in handcuffs, escorted by two policemen. He had been picked up for shoplifting in an electronics store.

Unaware of Danny's arrest, April stood calmly in front of Chief Sterns' desk. The big man was fuming, showing the side of himself that he kept hidden when the TV cameras were rolling.

'Just what is it you hoped to accomplish out there?' he demanded. 'Besides busting my chops, that is!'

April kept her composure. 'My friends in Little Tokyo have told me about this Foot Clan, Chief. I think you've heard as much about it as I have. And I don't think you're doing anything about it.'

Chief Sterns' eyebrows knotted together like battling caterpillars. 'You expect me to waste precious manpower because a few immigrants are reminded of something that supposedly happened years ago? In *Japan*?'

April nodded. 'If you have nothing else to go on, why not?'

Sterns half rose to his feet, banging the desktop angrily. 'Are you trying to tell me how to do my job?' he grated.

April smiled. 'Someone ought to.'

Sterns' face was red with rage. 'Out!' he bellowed. 'Get out of my office, O'Neil!'

The door slammed loudly as April walked back across to her crew. The sound of muffled swearing could be heard from inside the Chief's office.

The technician checked his watch. 'You were in there one minute seven seconds, Miss O'Neil,' he said with a grin.

'A new record,' April replied, laughing.

7

April hurried down the subway steps. Her vw van was still at the studio parking lot, since she had travelled to City Hall for the interview in the outside broadcast truck with the rest of the crew. As it was getting late, she decided to travel by train and pick it up the next day. That way she could avoid the aggravation of the rush-hour traffic.

She reached the platform just as the train pulled away. April gave a gasp of irritation and glared at her watch. That gave her another six minutes until the next one. She started to move over to a bench.

She was still mulling over her interview with Sterns. To April's way of thinking, he obviously knew more than he was letting on. But was he incompetent, or frightened to act . . . or was his involvement more sinister than that?

The figure who crept up behind her might have been reading her mind. 'Chief Sterns isn't the only one annoyed by your line of questioning, Miss O'Neil,' whispered a voice.

April spun round. She was confronted by a group of five men clad in black jumpsuits and balaclavas. They looked like they had strayed out of a bad martial arts movie, but the stance and tone of voice were real and threatening enough. She glanced up and down along the platform, but there was no-one else in sight.

The leader spoke again. 'We've been looking for you.'

April had no trouble placing the accent. Japanese.

She mustered a brave face. 'What, am I behind on my video payments again?' she asked.

The leader of the ninja stepped closer until his face was only inches from April's. 'Your mouth may yet bring you much trouble, Miss O'Neil,' he said softly. His gloved hand came up, clenched, in front of her. 'I deliver a message . . .'

He slowly uncurled his fingers, but the palm was empty. April looked on for a half-second before she understood what he meant to do. By that time it was too late to react. The ninja swung his hand, delivering two hard slaps on each side of her face.

'. . . Keep your mouth shut!'

Staggered, April realized they were moving to surround her. She was quite sure that the two slaps were not the only warning she would get. The ninja intended to give her a serious beating.

She remembered the strange dagger in her bag. But as she fumbled with it, one of the ninja delivered a roundhouse kick that swept it right out of her hand. The sai fell several feet away by a pillar on the platform. Unseen by April – or her attackers – a green hand slowly reached out and grabbed the sai . . .

Another of the ninja grabbed her from behind and pushed her forward roughly. April stumbled, losing a shoe. As they began to shove her around, she felt panic and anger building inside her in equal measure.

The anger won out. 'All right, that's *it*!' she yelled, lashing out at one of the ninja with her purse and landing a solid clout with it. He backed off, clutching a growing bump on his head, and April took full advantage of their surprise to flail at a couple of the others.

Unfortunately they were too well trained for her. A fourth ninja seized her and the leader stepped forward, his eyes blazing behind his black mask.

April saw his fist shoot towards her like a piledriver. Then she felt herself crumple to the ground . . .

The ninja stood over their fallen victim. The leader of the group raised his foot over her neck, poised for one more blow. It never landed.

Something heavy and green shot across the platform and struck the ninja in the midriff, bowling him over.

The other ninja moved in, thrown off-balance by the sudden arrival of this opponent in their midst. Raphael turned to face them. Slowly he sucked air into his lungs and adopted the double-weapon stance known as *happo biraki* – 'Alertness on All Eight Sides'. There was no easy opening for an attack against someone in this stance.

Either the ninja did not know that, or they were too fanatical to care. They darted forward in a black tide, and Raphael was forced to lash out in all directions to hold them back. Though heavily outnumbered, he fought like a cyclone. Gradually, pummelled and slashed, the Foot ninja fell back, giving Raphael enough space to haul April over his shoulder.

Heading for the edge of the platform, he heard the rails begin to rattle with the noise of an approaching train. A glance round confirmed that the ninja were in hot pursuit.

Raphael had nowhere else to go – he jumped down and began crossing the tracks. The ninja clustered at the edge of the platform to watch. Like lean grinning vultures, they were hoping for the worst.

The train pulled in and sped right through the station without stopping. The ninja waited, gleefully anticipating the blood of their foe on the rails. But when the carriages had all passed, there was no sign of Raphael or April.

Raphael glanced back from further along the tunnel. He had reached a maintenance recess just ahead of the train. By the time he emerged to scan the platform, the Foot ninja had vanished.

He turned and began to carry April up the dark tunnel.

He did not see the single ninja who emerged from behind a column and slipped like a silent shadow in pursuit . . .

8

'What – are you crazy, Raph?' said Leonardo, shaking his head dumbfounded as Raphael carefully lowered April's limp body on to their couch.

Raphael rounded on his brothers. He was confused and defensive. 'Yeah, Leo,' he snapped. 'I'm crazy, OK? I'm a total loonie – OK?'

The others crowded round. Michaelangelo in particular seemed mesmerized. He stared at April as though she were the princess in a fairytale. 'It's the newslady we saved the other night,' he breathed. 'Can we keep her?'

'Raph,' said Donatello, 'let me ask just one thing: *why?*'

That made Raphael stop and think. Even he was not quite sure why he'd brought April back to the den. But then, what else could he do? Leave her where the Foot might come back for her? Deliver her to Channel Three? Raphael set his jaw. No, he was sure he'd done the right thing.

'Why?' he said sarcastically. 'Why? Oh, I guess I just thought it was time we redecorated. You know, a couple o' throw pillows, a TV news reporter – what d'you *think*?'

There was the tap of a cane at the doorway. The Turtles froze and turned around. Master Splinter was standing there watching them.

'Raphael,' said the rat master of ninjutsu, 'what has happened?'

Raphael spread his hands imploringly. 'She got jumped in the subway, master. What else could I do? I had to bring her here . . .'

Splinter walked over to the couch, his progress followed by four pairs of anxious mutant eyes. But they were not the only ones watching. Behind a small vent high in the corner of the room, two more eyes stared for a moment before disappearing into the darkness.

Splinter and his pupils remained oblivious of the Foot spy. The aged rat touched April's forehead, then turned to the Turtles. 'Bring my herb jar,' he said. 'Cold washcloth. A pillow.'

Each request was directed at a different Turtle, and they all sprang gladly into action at their master's bidding. Meanwhile, Splinter sat down next to April and listened to Raphael's full story as he applied acupressure techniques to April's hands.

Her eyelids fluttered. 'Ah,' said Splinter. 'Our guest is beginning to come round . . .'

April heard his voice. It seemed to be echoing hollowly down a long tunnel. She fought her way to consciousness, feeling as though she were climbing out of a well of blackness.

Steadily the blackness melted away. April tentatively opened her eyes a crack. The next moment they popped open. She was staring up at a giant rat which loomed over her like every pest control man's worst nightmare!

'*Aieeee!*' she screamed.

The other three Turtles were on the far side of the room and had not seen April's coming around. Her scream so startled Leonardo that he dropped the herb jar, and Donatello almost jumped out of his shell.

April scrambled around so that her feet were up on the couch. Her fists were clenched defensively, and her lips twisted in horror. It was much the same posture as when the rat had frightened her in the studio parking lot. Except that, in this case, the giant size of the rat made her action pointless. Splinter could easily climb up on the couch beside her if he wanted to.

When she realized this – and saw that the giant rat was not about to attack – she relaxed a little. 'Right, like *this* is gonna do me a lot of good,' she muttered under her breath.

Her self control lasted only a second. At a cheerful 'Hi' she turned to see Michaelangelo standing right behind the couch.

'Ahhhh!' she shrieked.

Michaelangelo was almost as scared himself by the noise. He could hardly believe April's slight frame could house such a powerful set of lungs. He took a step back and tripped over the edge of the rug.

April's screaming died away to a confused babble. 'Oh my God, oh my God,' she kept saying. 'I'm dead. I must be dead. No, no – I'm dreaming. That's it, I'm dreaming.'

'No, you're not,' protested Donatello.

April was undeterred. She started to work it out to herself: 'Those guys in the black pyjamas hit me. I'm unconscious. I saw that rat before – that explains you . . .' She turned from Splinter to the Turtles. 'But *you* guys, I have *no* idea where you came from. Unless from something I glimpsed when those muggers were taken down in the parking lot. But that can't be it, because I was awake then . . .' She grabbed her head in both hands and shook it.

'You're awake now,' insisted Donatello.

Splinter's soothing voice cut through the confusion. 'If you will please just sit down and calm yourself, I will tell you where we came from.'

Splinter gently offered her his hand. April stared at it absently. A moment later she took it and sank back on the couch.

'It's really quite simple, Miss O'Neil . . .' began Splinter.

April shook her head. 'And it knows my name.

Perfect . . . Why couldn't I have a dream about Harrison Ford?'

Splinter went on. 'For fifteen years now we have lived here. Before that time I was an ordinary rat – the pet of Master Yoshi, an expert in the martial art of ninjutsu. I learned the secrets of the ninja by mimicking his movements from my cage. When we were forced to come to New York . . .' Splinter paused, a painful memory forcing him to blink, '. . . After we came to New York, my master was killed. For the first time I found myself without a home – without a family. I wandered the streets and sewers, foraging what food I could find.'

The Turtles settled back. They had heard this tale many times before, but they never tired of hearing it again. It told the story of their origins.

'And then, one day,' Splinter continued, 'I saw an old blind man crossing the street, unaware of the truck barrelling down upon him. Luckily a brave young man was standing on the kerb. Without hesitation, he dived and pushed the old man out of the way, but not before the truck driver had violently swerved. A metal canister was dislodged from the truck and struck a glass jar held by an onlooker's little boy – a jar containing four baby turtles.'

'That was us,' whispered Michaelangelo.

'Shh!' hissed his brothers, rapt in attention.

'The jar broke and the little ones fell into a man-hole, followed by the canister. It smashed open in the fall and they were covered in a glowing ooze.

I know this, because I saw it happen and was on hand to help them. I cleaned the ooze off them and gathered them together in a discarded coffee jar.'

Michaelangelo rubbed his hands, scarcely daring to take a breath. He loved the next bit best of all.

'When I awoke the next morning,' said Splinter, 'the jar was tipped over. They had doubled in size! And I, too, was growing – particularly in intellect, though my stature never matched theirs. Soon they began to stand upright, copying my every movement. I was amazed at how intelligent they seemed. But nothing could prepare me for what happened next: one of them spoke!'

'Me,' put in Michaelangelo. 'I said "pizza", didn't I, master?' The others shushed him again.

'More words followed,' explained Splinter, 'and then I began their training, teaching them all that I had learned from Master Yoshi. With a battered copy of an art book that I had salvaged from the storm drains, I named them . . .'

The aged rat turned and proudly gestured to each of his pupils in turn. 'Leonardo . . .'

Leonardo straightened his back and bowed in the Japanese fashion.

'. . . Michaelangelo . . .'

Mike anxiously pointed to himself in case April should miss him.

'. . . Donatello . . .'

Donatello shrugged, slightly embarrassed.

'. . . and Raphael.'

Raphael leaned against the wall, nonchalantly picking at his teeth with the prong of a sai.

April sat spellbound on the couch. For some time she could not collect her thoughts enough to say anything. She swallowed long and hard. Surely this couldn't be happening . . .? Four mutant turtles and a giant rat stepfather? It sounded like something out of a rather daft fairytale.

Finally she pinched herself and was alarmed to find that it hurt.

'So,' she said, 'I'm not dreaming after all.'

9

After some argument, April finally agreed to let the Turtles escort her home. Splinter had pointed out that The Foot would not be deterred by one setback, and that the ideal way for April to return to her apartment in safety was to take the sewer route.

As the Turtles led her through a maze of tunnels, April took a glance down at the mucky stuff sloshing around her Italian leather boots and gave a sigh. That was two hundred dollars down the drain, so to speak – but on reflection it was better to have her shoes ruined than her face.

'Are you guys sure you know where you're going?' she asked dubiously. The Turtles may have lived down here all their lives, but all these tunnels looked the same.

'Eleventh and Bleecker?' confirmed Michaelangelo. He paused and sniffed the air. 'Hmm, this smells more like Ninth Street. A bit further.'

The others smiled at April. Michaelangelo was trying to put her at her ease in the best way he knew — by kidding around. Unfortunately, still shaken by her encounter with The Foot, and dazed by her encounter with the Turtles, April was in no mood for jocularity.

Michaelangelo gave a shrug and turned away to lead on down the tunnel.

Finally they reached the intersection of Eleventh Street and Bleecker, where April's apartment building was situated. After lifting the manhole cover and taking a peek to ensure that no-one was about, Donatello scrambled through and reached down to help April up.

An awkward moment went by. April had no idea what to say.

'Well . . .' she ventured. 'I guess I'd invite you all in . . . but the place is a real mess.'

'That's OK!' piped up Michaelangelo from the open manhole.

April spread her hands. 'Well . . . and I really don't have anything to offer you. I don't know what turtles like, come to that. The only thing I have in is frozen pizza . . .'

'Pizza? Let's go for it!'

There was a green blur as Michaelangelo jumped up beside Donatello. He was quickly followed by the other two.

'You said the magic word,' Donatello told April with an apologetic grin.

Not for the first time that night, April was taken aback. 'You guys eat *pizza*?'

Now it was Michaelangelo's turn to look astonished. 'Doesn't everybody?' he said.

'Well . . . yeah, but . . .' April had no real answer to that. 'All right,' she conceded.

When they got up to the apartment, the Turtles momentarily forgot about pizza. 'Just look at this pad!' said Michaelangelo, awed. In comparison to their subterranean den, April's place was the pinnacle of luxury.

Donatello immediately found a few comic books that Danny Pennington had left behind. He stretched out on the sofa and began reading them.

Leonardo and Raphael, meanwhile, had discovered the aquarium and were delightedly pointing out various kinds of tropical fish. 'Splinter says that watching fish is sort of like meditation,' announced Michaelangelo.

April looked at them and shook her head, but there was a smile on her lips. The Turtles had a way of making themselves at home that helped restore her nerves after the evening's excitement.

'So,' she said, 'what do you guys like on your pizza?'

'Oh, just the regular stuff,' Michaelangelo told her. 'You know – flies, stinkbugs, slugs . . .'

April was halfway to the kitchen. She froze in horror.

'Just a joke,' explained Michaelangelo. 'Pepperoni and olives will do just fine.'

April gave a relieved laugh. She realized that Turtle humour was going to take some getting used to.

A half hour later, surrounded by mostly eaten pizza remnants, she was well into her initiation. Michaelangelo was doing a string of hilarious impersonations which had her rocking uncontrollably with laughter.

Curling his lip, Michaelangelo showed her his mimicking of Sylvester Stallone: ''Ey, yo, wuh maybe I'll fight Apollo Creed, an' maybe I won't. What d'*you* think – Adriaaan.'

April roared in hysterics. She really wanted Michaelangelo to stop so she could catch her breath, but he ploughed straight on into an imitation of Cagney:

'Ah, you dirty rat. You killed my brother. You dirty rat.'

'Ha ha!' gasped April. 'That must be Splinter's favourite!'

She laughed again, but the Turtles hesitated. Had she just cracked a . . .

'It was a joke,' April told them with a wink. And the Turtles knew that they'd just made their first human friend.

Ever dutiful, Leonardo realized that they ought to be getting back home. 'Speaking of Master

Splinter, we should be going,' he announced, getting up. 'He worries about us.'

'Well,' said April, seeing them out, 'I don't know what to say. Will I ever see you guys again, do you think?' For once she wasn't thinking as a reporter on the trail of a scoop. She had genuinely enjoyed the Turtles' company.

Leonardo gave her an OK sign as they walked off down the corridor. 'That depends on how fast you restock your pizza!' he called back.

Without April to slow them up, the Turtles made much better time getting back. They jogged along the tunnels, sloshing uncaringly through muck and slime, until they reached the door of their den.

'No doubt about it,' Leonardo was saying, 'she loved us.'

Michaelangelo agreed. 'It was my impressions that broke the ice,' he claimed.

Donatello gave a snort. 'Dream on, bro'!'

Raphael, in the lead, suddenly stopped dead. There was something wrong with the door. It looked more broken-up than usual. 'Hold it!' he hissed.

The Turtles dropped their carefree teen personas. Now they were four alert ninja with razor-keen fighting instincts. Their weapons were readied in an instant.

Taking a cautious step forward, Raphael eased

open the door. They looked through, and their jaws dropped open in horror.

The den had been completely smashed up, apparently in a ferocious struggle. All their salvaged gear – the ghetto blaster, telephone booth and so on – lay in wrecked fragments around the floor.

There was no sign of their master.

Raphael rushed over to Splinter's empty chair. A dark streak stained the seat. He hardly dared to reach out his fingers and touch it. It was moist and red. Splinter's blood.

Raphael's forlorn howl of anguish ripped through the darkness of the sewers like a knife.

10

Charles Pennington was having a bad day. And it was only 7.30 A.M.

The previous evening, his son Danny had been arrested for shoplifting in an electronics store. Charles gave him a good ticking off after paying his bail, and he had thought that was pretty much the end of the matter. A man with his wealth and standing should have little trouble dealing with a shoplifting offence. Perhaps he could put pressure on the store to drop charges – maybe in exchange for an advertising concession?

Then Charles' phone had rung first thing in the morning, and he had realized that his position also laid him open to having others put pressure on *him*.

It was Chief Sterns calling. He had seen the arrest report on Danny. He made his voice sound full of concern, but Charles was left in no doubt of the real reason for the call. When Sterns alluded to April's 'unprofessional' reporting of the 'so-called' crime wave, Charles knew what he was being told:

Get April O'Neil to ease off – *or else*.

Charles called by April's apartment first thing to break the news to her. He did not much like interfering with his reporters' editorial freedom – and he knew April was a first-rate reporter – but he had to put his family and his reputation first. He felt slightly sick as he pressed the doorbell.

Inside, April was talking with the Turtles. Having nowhere else to go when they had got back to find Splinter missing, they had naturally turned to their only friend. After a fretful night, they were lying around her apartment in despondent mood.

The sound of the bell made them all jump. April went over to the door and, clearing her throat, did her best to sound unperturbed: 'Who is it?'

'It's me – Charles. C'mon, April . . .'

April pressed her hand to her head. 'Oh no!' she whispered through gritted teeth. 'It's my boss. Can you guys . . .'

She turned round. There was no sign of the Turtles.

'. . . hide . . .?' she finished, amazed. Even though she knew the Turtles were still in the apartment, she couldn't spot them. Obviously there really was something to the ninja 'art of invisibility'.

Throwing on a robe, she opened the door. 'Charles,' she said, affecting a nonchalant tone of voice. 'What's up? Are you going to make a habit of calling on me first thing in the mornings?'

Charles shuffled past her into the room followed by his son. April could see he looked worn and harried, and for some reason he avoided looking her straight in the eye. As he began to mumble a half-prepared speech, she got a bad feeling about the reason for his visit.

'April, listen,' he said. 'I've, uh, been thinking . . . you know, you've, uh, been working awful hard on this story lately. Maybe you should take it easy for a while. Let somebody else handle it . . . you know, just for a little while.'

April's premonition was confirmed. She immediately went on the defensive. 'Charles, what are you talking about?' she demanded. 'This is *my* story. No way am I handing it to anyone else.'

While Danny meandered disinterestedly around the room, absently examining various objects, Charles finally noticed how dishevelled April was looking.

It was like a lifeline to a drowning man. 'But, I mean, *look* at you,' he countered. 'You're exhausted.'

April turned on her heel and headed to the bathroom to freshen up. 'I just had a rough night.'

As she started to splash cold water over her face, Charles followed after her. 'Well,' he went on, 'at least let someone help you with . . . I don't know, with covering City Hall, for instance.'

Michaelangelo, hidden behind the sofa, chose

this moment to take a peek out. He was reasonably certain that no one was looking in his direction. But he was unaware of Danny, who was standing in front of a mirror and was utterly awestruck to catch a glimpse of what looked like a bald green head poking up from behind the sofa. The boy froze for an instant, then whirled. Michaelangelo ducked down with precise timing, so that by the time Danny had turned round he was no longer in sight.

Danny blinked, shook his head, then took a second glance back in the mirror. Nothing. While he was trying to work out what had made him imagine seeing a green-skinned alien out of one of his comic books, Michaelangelo scarpered unseen behind a different piece of furniture.

April, meanwhile, was getting increasingly exasperated with her boss's evasive arguments. 'Charles, just what's with you today?' she asked.

Charles covered his embarrassment with a pretence of injured pride. 'Nothing's "with me" today. I just thought you might like a little help, that's all. Sheesh, can't a boss show a little concern for his team once in a while?'

'Thanks for the concern, but I *don't* need any help,' said April firmly, raising her head from the basin. 'Besides,' she added, 'I think Sterns gets on well with me.'

Charles mimed 'oh sure' while April felt around for something to dry her face.

'Hand me a towel, will you?' she said.

He looked around 'Where do you keep them . . .?'

As he put his hand on the edge of the shower curtain to look behind it, April caught a sudden glimpse of a green shell on the other side.

'Charles, no —' she gasped.

It was too late. Charles jerked the curtain back. The shower was empty.

He turned to her with a bemused expression. 'April? What's wrong?'

Donatello was braced across the top of the shower, out of Charles' line of sight. April hurried over, grabbed a towel from the rack above the shower, and whipped the curtain across again.

'Wrong?' She tried to think of something. 'Well . . . now you've gone and seen my unsightly bath-tub ring!'

Charles gaped at her in amazement. He had only intended the overwork thing as an excuse to take her off reporting at City Hall, but April's weird behaviour was getting him genuinely worried. Maybe she really *did* need a holiday.

April started shepherding him through the apartment to the front door. 'C'mon, Charles, out of here. Out! Out! I have to get ready for work . . .'

She noticed Danny peering with a perplexed expression behind the sofa where he had caught a glimpse of Michaelangelo. 'Hey, Danny,' she called out, 'tell your dad to relax.'

Danny glanced round and raised his eyebrows. 'I *wish*.'

He headed out of the door behind his father, who shot him a look before adding one last thing to April. 'Just . . . don't push any buttons today, OK?'

April closed the door and stared at it for a moment with knitted brows. Charles was definitely not himself today. She couldn't figure out why he was trying to steer her slant on the story, though. She had thought he shared her concern at the police chief's ineptitude.

A voice broke into April's reverie: 'That was close.' Startled, she almost bumped her head on the door in her haste to turn round.

The Turtles were emerging from their ingenious hiding-places all around the apartment. Michael-angelo, standing right at April's shoulder, noticed her shaken expression. 'Really, April,' he admonished. 'It's time you switched to decaf.'

Once he got back down to his car, Charles had had time to think about what he was doing. He was trying to warn one of his reporters off a perfectly respectable approach to a story. He was disgusted at himself.

Since Danny was the reason that Chief Sterns had leverage on him in the first place, he took out his frustration on his son.

'I just don't get it, Danny,' he said, glaring over the steering-wheel at the early morning traffic. 'I make enough money to give you everything a kid could want – and yet you're out stealing. Why?'

Danny stared sullenly ahead. 'I don't know,' he murmured.

'You don't know. What the hell were you going to do with a car stereo, anyway? Or don't you know *that* either?'

'Sorry.'

'Sorry!' Charles exploded in fury. 'Not as sorry as you're *going* to be after school . . .'

He glanced up at a red light. The car screeched to a halt.

Without even a glance at his father, Danny jerked open his door and took off at a run.

'Danny! Danny!' Charles pulled into the intersection to make a right turn after the fleeing boy. A car swerved and immediately there was a cacophony of blaring horns. Charles pulled over to the kerb and caught a last glimpse of Danny vanishing down a narrow alleyway.

There was a tap at the car window. A traffic cop. As Charles wound down the window, the cop was already writing out a ticket. His day was going from bad to worse.

11

Tatsu walked into his master's warehouse and surveyed the scene through grimly slitted eyes.

Tatsu was a bald, burly man dressed in a black martial arts *dogi* adorned with a red dragon emblem. This uniform marked him as second-in-command of The Foot Clan ninja, whose training began and ended in this very warehouse. Here, in the heart of Brooklyn, disaffected youths could be recruited to the organization. Once trained to use the ninja skills of speed and stealth to nefarious ends, they were sent out into the city. There they put their skills to good use, perpetrating a unique kind of crime wave.

A *silent* crime wave.

The first area of the warehouse was 'Pleasure Island'. This was where newcomers to the organization were left to their own devices. They enjoyed playing pool and video games, gambling, smoking and generally hanging out. It was the antidote to the responsible ways of life that their parents had tried to force on them. Here, the insistent stricture 'You can't do that' was never heard. These kids were given free rein.

Tatsu nodded to himself and passed on. His bulldog features remained creased in a glowering frown, but the eyes showed a gleam of satisfaction. Once those youngsters had enjoyed themselves to the full, once they had shaken off the vestiges of a law-abiding past, once the scruples carefully instilled by their parents had been stripped away – then they could begin their training as Foot ninja.

As Tatsu made his way out of the 'Pleasure Island' area, a youngster who was not watching where he partied bumped into him. He turned and looked up at Tatsu.

Tatsu stared back. For an instant his eyes were full of thunder, like the rain dragon of Oriental myth that he was named after. The boy swallowed hard and took a half step backwards before fear took the strength out of his legs. He was conscious of being very fragile and vulnerable beside the massive ninja warrior.

Tatsu experienced a moment of anger, but it evaporated. Only the inferior man wastes effort disciplining an unintended slight, he reminded himself. Forcing his harsh features into the closest they could approach to a smile, he gave a gesture of dismissal with his fingers.

'Go,' he grunted. 'Play.'

The youth did not need telling twice. With a smile of relief, he ran back to rejoin his friends.

Tatsu walked on past high stacks of boxes. Many were open, and most were covered with camouflage netting and drapes. They contained any contraband that could be pocketed, carried or driven to the warehouse. These boxes contained those ill-gotten gains which were distributed back to the organization's members as bonuses.

At the back of this area was a secluded alcove partitioned off by a locked gate covered with netting. A line of crates concealed it from casual glances. Tatsu looked towards it with a sneer. He did not need to include the alcove in his tour of inspection, since he had only recently come from interrogating the prisoner who hung in manacles there.

It was a very strange prisoner indeed – some kind of mutant rat. Tatsu gave a barely perceptible shrug. Whatever lay behind such a mystery, it would soon be solved by the implacable intellect of his master, the Shredder. Tatsu had other, more mundane, matters to attend to. He turned away from the alcove entrance.

Across a catwalk connecting the two elevated side levels of the vast warehouse, Tatsu entered the novice training area. There were no videos or pool tables here, and in place of dance music came the grunts of energetic exercise.

This was where the budding ninja received the

first level of instruction. Such novices in ninjutsu were called *kusa*. They were given dragon-printed headbands and let loose on an array of bars, hoops, ropes, ladders and climbing frames. The youths here were fewer in number than those in the first area, but they seemed to be having just as much fun. The difference was that none of them were smoking or drinking. They looked much fitter than the raw recruits, as they got their enjoyment from competition in healthy exercise.

An older teen dressed in a black ninja suit acted as instructor. As Tatsu approached, he blew a whistle and timed a number of youths as they climbed ropes to the ceiling.

They ascended fast, then dropped deftly back down to the floor. The instructor flicked his stopwatch as the last foot touched the ground.

Tatsu took hold of his wrist and inspected the stopwatch. He reacted with a slight shake of the head and a brusque grunt. *Not good enough yet*, was what the instructor understood by this: *train them harder*.

Tatsu moved on to watch the classic pickpocket exercise: a stuffed dummy adorned with numerous bells. Around the dummy were gathered a group of eager teenagers. Their instructor — again, a somewhat older youth — threw a smoke pellet at the dummy's feet as he started his stopwatch.

The boys rushed into the cloud of smoke as it billowed up. Faint half-glimpsed flurries of motion indicated their actions, but no sound could be heard.

When the smoke cleared, the dummy had been stripped of its bells.

Tatsu stepped in to inspect the dummy. Lifting its arm, he revealed a single bell that the novices had overlooked. He ripped it away from its stitching and, glaring at them, gave it a single *ding*.

'More practice,' he commanded tersely, tossing the bell to the instructor as he continued on.

The next area was where the training became a serious business. There was no laughter, no cheerful sport, just deadly serious young men in black ninja *dogi*. They knelt around a large mat watching two youths locked in unarmed combat. The fighters were using karate for the most part, plus various tricks culled from other martial arts. But there was a difference.

In normal karate the blows are pulled a split-second before they land. These youths, however, were fighting for real.

The taller and stronger of the two was clearly superior. He was already getting the upper hand as Tatsu walked up to the edge of the mat. Now, seeing the arrival of the senior instructor, he tore into his opponent with hard slugging punches. In seconds the other youth was knocked down on the mat, where he lay stunned until two other trainees ran in to drag his senseless form away.

Tatsu nodded and gave a grunt of approval. Keeping his eyes on the winner, he stepped out on to the mat and assumed a ready combat stance.

Suddenly, without even the flutter of an eyelid to give warning, he lashed out at the youth. Explosive *ki-ai* shouts echoed through the warehouse.

The youth fell back, blocking each of Tatsu's lightning-swift attacks. After half a minute of this, Tatsu ceased his assault. 'Very good,' he conceded, standing back and bowing to his opponent.

The youth smiled and returned the gesture. The instant he lowered his eyes, Tatsu swung a vicious uppercut right in his face, bowling him over on to his back. Before the youth could recover, Tatsu dropped so that one knee pressed down on his chest. A knife, drawn from some concealed sheath, pricked the skin of the youth's throat.

'*Never* lower your eyes to a foe,' Tatsu said fiercely.

The youth stared up in terror. For all his skill on the practice mat, he had never truly faced death before. He nodded vigorously.

Tatsu stood, letting his victim up, and put away his dagger just as a dull tone sounded throughout the warehouse. It was the assembly bell. As it repeated, teenagers filed from every part of the building. A whisper of excitement went up:

The Shredder was coming.

12

Danny Pennington had been found on the streets by two slightly older boys who brought him to the warehouse. He had never heard of the Shredder, and he was not clear what being a member of The Foot would entail, but he knew straightaway he saw the ranks of video games that he was in paradise.

He spent the first day playing to his heart's content. He didn't think of his father once, except as a vague nagging presence that had been lifted from him. He had no idea what the later instalments of ninja training involved, but he could handle any amount of playing pool and reading comic books.

When the assembly gong went, Danny did not know what it meant. He took his cue from the other youngsters, who hastily left off whatever they were doing and headed for the centre of the warehouse.

The railings overlooking the assembly area soon filled with eager teenagers, all bristling with anticipation as they looked down to the ground level below. There, a group of older youths in black *dogi* silently moved into formation. They stood very erect, silent and still.

Danny's eyes widened in excitement. With training, he would learn to be one of those ninja. He would earn his Foot *dogi*! He forgot all about the comic books and video games. He could hardly wait for training to begin.

The low, insistent tones of the assembly gong faded away, leaving an abrupt hush to settle over everyone present. For a moment, no-one so much as drew breath.

A shaft of light stabbed out through the dusty air as a door opened at the far end of the warehouse. All eyes turned. A shadow appeared in the light, growing longer and longer as the figure approached the centre of the chamber.

As the figure passed from shadow into light, burnished glints picked out the metal helmet that covered his head. Only the figure's dark, intense eyes were visible through the helmet's visor. His black cloak billowed and swayed as he strode forward to the centre of the warehouse.

The silence became too much. Gradually Danny became aware of a whisper buzzing around among the new recruits:

'*The Shredder . . !*'

Below, the Shredder swept on imperiously toward the centre of the floor. He looked neither right nor left, but stared intently ahead as he walked in a way that conveyed the absoluteness of his character better than any words.

Tatsu came forward and bowed. As the Shredder waited as motionless as an ice sculpture, he carefully removed his master's long cloak.

The reason for his care became evident as the cloak was swept away to reveal the Shredder's garb. Over his severe black *dogi*, he wore metal ninja armour that bristled with razor-sharp spikes.

Looking off to one side, Tatsu issued a curt command. Four teenagers edged nervously forward into the light. They were the same thugs who had attacked April in the studio parking lot when she stumbled across their robbery – and who had subsequently been beaten by the Turtles.

Next, Tatsu produced an ornate red headband which he proceeded to drape over the Shredder's shoulder. He gestured to the four boys, who responded by shuffling into a circle around the armoured ninja lord. There was no trace of their customary swaggering bravado now. They just looked sick with fear.

Another gesture from Tatsu, and a *dogi*-clad attendant came forward with weapons for the four youths. The Shredder had no weapon, and still he remained immobile. His eyes glittered unblinkingly behind the metal visor.

The youths took the weapons with perspiring hands. The test was to see whether any of them could take the headband. The one who succeeded in this would not receive a reward, however. Rather, he would avoid punishment.

Tatsu stepped away. As he raised his hand, absolute silence fell over the audience of trainee ninja. Everyone watched Tatsu's hand.

The hand dropped, closing into a fist. At this signal the four youths lunged in to the attack, desperation overcoming their fear. Their attempts were to no avail. It was as if the Shredder knew in advance where each was going to strike. With economical movements – never making a sound, never wasting a motion – he blocked every attack. And as he did, he used the spikes on his armour to slash each youth in turn. Applying a surgeon's precision, he placed one scarlet tear across a shoulder, another wound to the stomach . . . until all four of the youths stood panting and bleeding around him.

They were helped away by other Foot members while Tatsu retrieved the red headband from the Shredder's shoulder.

Now, finally, the Shredder spoke. It was a chilling sound – the voice of a man without emotion, echoing tinnily inside the blank faceplate of his armour:

'Money, paid as bail for your freedom, is money lost to The Foot. Now these four have paid their debt. Their punishment was just, as it always is in

84

our family. They will wear their scars proudly as reminders of their quest to become *full* members of The Foot.'

He extended a hand as his words reverberated around the cavernous interior of the warehouse. With a slight nod and a narrowing of the eyes, he signalled to a *dogi*-garbed teenager who had been waiting off to one side. The teenager approached and knelt at his master's feet.

'That's Shinsho,' whispered a boy standing next to Danny. 'This is his, like, graduation.'

Tatsu reached out and placed a black hood into the Shredder's hand. Slowly, with ceremonial gravity, the ninja lord lowered it over the young initiate's head. Shinsho gave a deep bow and, rising, returned to his place. Now he was a full-fledged member of the clan. He could sense the envious looks of the recruits, and under his hood he beamed with pride.

The Shredder's voice rang out again. 'Our family grows. Soon we will break the confines of these walls. The city itself shall be our playground, to use as we please . . . rewarding ourselves . . . punishing our enemies.'

He looked up and scanned the assemblage before continuing: 'But there is a new enemy. Freaks of nature who interfere with our business. You are my eyes and ears. Find them. Together we shall punish these creatures, these . . . turtles.'

Turtles!? Danny remembered the weird figure he had seen in April's apartment. Yeah, that's just what it had looked like – some kind of giant turtle. Before he quite realized what he was doing, he started to raise his hand.

No-one noticed, so Danny pushed forward to the rail with his hand up. The other youngsters nearby edged away. They thought Danny must be crazy, and they didn't want anything to do with him.

The Shredder turned his head. As his eyes locked on Danny, he could see the earnest look on his face. As a trained ninja, he could read much from a person's expression. Incredible as it seemed, this boy had information about the Turtles.

Behind his metal faceplate, the Shredder smiled.

13

Unable to snap out of their depression at Splinter's disappearance, the Turtles had done nothing for days but lounge around April's apartment. As Michaelangelo flipped between quiz shows, soaps and old *Kung Fu* repeats, he suddenly gave a yelp of surprise.

'Hey, you guys!' he called. 'It's April.'

April was sitting behind a news desk on the Eyewitness News programme being interviewed by a fellow reporter. For a moment the Turtles' despondency was forgotten as they gathered round to hear her describing how she had been attacked in the subway.

'A *"dogi"*?' the other reporter was saying. 'What's that?'

'It's a Japanese word,' April explained. 'I've been doing a little research, and that's the name for the type of jumpsuit my attackers wore. It's like martial arts gear.'

Donatello nodded his approval. 'Boy, she's smart.'

'She's a good reporter,' agreed Leonardo.

'She's a *babe*,' announced Michaelangelo breathlessly.

'Keep it down, willya?' growled Raphael. 'Let's hear what they say.'

The other reporter had just made some comment on the subway attack. April nodded vigorously. '. . . Exactly, June,' she continued. 'This was no ordinary mugging; they were trying to warn me off. I'm convinced that these men were affiliated to a clandestine organization known as The Foot.'

The other reporter, June, raised her eyebrows. 'Excuse me . . . The "Foot"?'

April spread her hands. 'Yeah, I know, it sounds more like a nightclub for chiropodists than a sinister criminal gang. But I've spoken with a lot of Japanese-Americans in the past few days. They say that our recent crime wave here in New York is reminiscent of a secret band of "ninja" thieves who once operated in Tokyo.'

'Are the authorities looking into this?'

'Well, June, I included everything in my statement to the police, but I doubt that Chief Sterns . . .' April looked directly into the camera at this point '. . . is taking the possible connection seriously.'

Charles Pennington, standing behind one of the cameras, winced. This was just the kind of thing he had hoped April would avoid. His headache got a lot worse a few seconds later, when a secretary gestured him over to the studio door. 'Mr Pennington, sir,' she said quietly. 'There's a telephone call for you; it's City Hall.'

'. . . If any of our viewers have further information about The Foot – ,' June was saying, '– or about the current spate of crimes, perhaps they'll get in touch with either the police or with us here on Channel Three News.' She turned back to April. 'I've got one last question, April – you still haven't told us how you managed to get away from those muggers?'

'Well,' said April after a pause, 'that's because I'm not sure that anyone would believe me. It's really quite incredible . . .'

In the apartment, the Turtles sat to shocked attention. Surely she wasn't going to break her word and tell about them?

They need not have worried. April was wise enough to tell just part of the truth. '. . . A citizen of New York City actually came to my rescue.'

'And who says chivalry is dead?' put in June. They both laughed.

'. . . But seriously,' added April, 'I'd like to take this opportunity to thank that gallant individual. If he's watching . . .' She turned to face the camera and gave a wink. '. . . Thanks, Raphael.'

'Wooooooo . . .' teased the other Turtles in unison.

Raphael squirmed in his chair.

'Hey, look,' said Donatello, pointing, 'he's going red!'

Raphael's eyes flashed with annoyance. He hated his brothers to poke fun at him. 'I am not!' he snapped.

Donatello was undeterred. 'I think he is!' he persisted. 'He's blushing!'

One of Raphael's sais shot through the air and stuck in the floor right between Donatello's legs.

'Then again . . .' said Donatello, pursing his lips . . . 'maybe not.'

Raphael was keen to change the subject. 'So what do we do now?'

'What do you mean?' said Leonardo, clicking off the television. 'What can we do now?'

Raphael jumped to his feet and pointed out of the window. 'Look, Leo – *Splinter's* out there somewhere!'

Leonardo followed the direction of Raphael's finger. It was a big city. He just shook his head. 'I *know* that,' he said, 'but we've got no way of finding him.'

'We could at least try!' shouted Raphael.

As the volume of the argument rose to a full-scale row, Michaelangelo and Donatello exchanged a glance and then crept off into the kitchen to raid the refrigerator.

'We can't do anything, Raph,' said Leonardo firmly. 'April's our only link to those guys. We'll have to wait until she turns up something.'

'Oh, *right*!' sneered Raphael. 'So *that's* the plan

from our "great leader", huh? Just sit here on our *butts*!'

'I never said I was your "great leader",' said Leonardo, losing his temper.

'Well, you sure *act* like it sometimes!'

'Yeah? Well, you act like a *jerk* sometimes, you know that? And this attitude problem of yours isn't helping anything!'

For Raphael that was the last straw. He grabbed up his sai and stormed over to the door. 'Well, maybe I'll just take my "attitude" and leave!'

Leonardo knew he shouldn't have snapped at his brother, but he was too full of anger himself to be repentant. 'So what's stopping you?' he demanded.

'Don't *worry*,' said Raphael. 'I'm gone!'

Leonardo had to have the last word. As Raphael flung the door open, he called out, 'Go ahead! We don't need you!'

He regretted saying it the instant the door slammed shut. This was a time that the Turtles needed one another most of all. He just hoped that Raphael would realize that, too, and that he would come back once he'd let off some steam.

14

It was only once he had slammed the door shut behind him that it occurred to Raphael that he had nowhere to go. In his anger, he hadn't even thought to bring his street disguise.

He glared back at the closed door. Going back now was out of the question. It would look like he was crawling back with his tail between his legs, and Raphael did not like to lose face. He'd go back when he was good and ready. First he needed a place to cool off.

He glanced along the corridor to the fire escape. Of course! If he couldn't go down on the street, he could go up to the roof. He could get a better perspective on things from up there, as well as clearing his head with a little fresh air. It might even help him think of an angle on how to trace Splinter's whereabouts.

*　　*　　*

A few blocks away, a similar idea had occurred to someone else. Casey Jones was reclining in an old deck-chair on the roof of his apartment building. He had a can of beer in one hand and a baseball bat in the other, which he tapped rhythmically on the leg of the deck-chair as he drank.

The rooftop overlooked most of the neighbouring buildings, giving a fine view right out across the city. It was a warm day, but there was only patchy sunshine, and enough of a breeze to deter anyone else from coming up.

Alone, Casey felt as though this was his domain. For a short space of time he felt contented. 'Top o' the world, ma!' he said to himself, grinning.

A movement, far off on another rooftop, made Casey sit up. It was something green, leaping from rooftop to rooftop in a way that seemed decidedly familiar. Casey squinted into the glare of sunshine half-covered by clouds. His suspicions were confirmed: it was the weird green stranger who had set upon him in the park a few nights before. Raphael, he had called himself – Casey would never forget that, to be sure, since he'd had it virtually beaten into him.

He hefted the bat and, tossing the crumpled beer can aside, reached for his hockey mask. He welcomed the chance to even the score between them.

Then Casey saw something else. There were a number of figures in black jumpsuits zigzagging across the rooftop behind Raphael. The Turtle did not seem to have noticed them yet, but they were signalling to each other. It was pretty obvious that they were getting ready to launch a sneak attack.

Casey scowled. He could count at least a dozen guys in black. Odds like that were just not fair. Casey caressed his bat as he looked for the quickest way over to the roof where Raphael was.

He was going to have to do something about evening out those odds.

The Foot attacked without mercy, without warning. Just as Tatsu had taught them.

Before he knew what was happening, Raphael was struck by a flying kick that flung him against a chimneystack. Stunned by the impact, he felt both sais drop from his hands.

One of the Foot ninja snatched them up and flung them over the edge of the roof. 'See how you manage without your weapons,' he hissed at Raphael.

Raphael rubbed the side of his head. He had a nasty lump forming where he had hit the bricks, but it was nothing compared to what he intended to dish out to these would-be ninja warriors now they had given him time to recover.

'Hey,' he said casually. 'I thought you guys always used the subway.'

Raphael knew that a taunting wisecrack was one of the best ways of provoking an opponent into attacking rashly. Five of the ninja ran forward one after the other – and came sailing back just as fast as Raphael laid into them with mammoth punches.

Two ninja threw a glance at one another, then tried rushing the Turtle simultaneously. Raphael flipped over into a handstand and sprang up, cannoning into them with a double kick before twisting around to land on his feet again.

The remaining Foot warriors hesitated.

Raphael gave a snort of derisive laughter. 'I mean, come *on* – you could learn better moves from a karate correspondence course. How do you jokers expect to beat me?'

As if on cue, grappling irons locked on to the side of the roof and a veritable legion of Foot ninja clambered up over the parapet.

Raphael sucked in a breath. 'Yeah, good answer, good answer . . .' he muttered. He felt a lot less cocksure now.

Beset on all sides, Raphael fought as well as he could. But he was soon hard pressed to defend himself, much less counterattack. Lashing out, he managed to connect with a few jaws, but the black-clad fighters were washing over him faster than he could knock them down. He was pummelled by blow after blow, until his guts felt like scrambled eggs and his eyes started to close up from livid swellings. All he could do was swing wildly. He had no time for jokes now; he was fighting for his life.

A manhole cover is silently removed by a powerfully-built, green figure – one of the Turtles ready for action

Raphael dons the standard Turtle disguise – trenchcoat and fedora – before heading out on to the streets

Casey Jones makes a stand against the crime wave

The Turtles rely on the wisdom and knowledge of their master, Splinter the rat

April learns that it's a lot of fun
being around the Turtles (above)
but none of them know of the
plans of the evil ninja
master of the Foot Clan, Shredder
(below)

While Leonardo checks out some of the objects in the junk shop below April's apartment (above), Raphael is taken by surprise on the rooftop by a Foot Clan attack (below)

Michaelangelo and Donatello dress a few of their wounds (above), while Leo keeps a vigil by the injured Raphael (below)

Donatello feels right at home
behind the wheel of the old pickup

Leonardo slips away to a quiet
spot to meditate

Leonardo shows his brothers a
new and radical way of fighting
(above) and the four Turtles begin
to practise the new skills (below)

Danny reluctantly reveals the Turtles' whereabouts to Shredder (above), and a fierce battle is soon underway (below)

A nunchuku swept around to strike him behind the knees, and he tumbled backwards. Snarling in anticipation of victory, the Foot ninja fell on their helpless victim. A brutal kick lashed down, slamming his head against the concrete roof.

Raphael's last thought as he lost consciousness was of Splinter – and that he had failed him . . .

Back at April's apartment the other Turtles, unaware of their brother's fate, were killing time until April got home. Michaelangelo and Donatello sat cross-legged on the floor in front of the television with a bag of nacho cheese doritos between them. Meanwhile Leonardo, brooding over his row with Raphael, paced restlessly up and down.

Michaelangelo, in his usual way, had got absorbed in the TV programme enough to put their troubles out of his mind for a while. 'Man,' he said through a mouthful of doritos, 'that Dino could really act! You know, bro', they should make this into a movie.'

'Right,' said Donatello sarcastically. 'Like, how are they gonna make a cartoon into a movie?'

Michaelangelo was mulling that one over as the key turned in the lock. All three were instantly on their guard, but it was only April.

'Hi, April,' said Michaelangelo. 'We saw you on TV. You were great!'

April gave him a big smile as she hung up her coat. 'Thanks, Mikie.'

Michaelangelo could hardly contain his joy. He

leaned closer to Donatello and whispered, 'Hear that? She called me *Mikie* . . .'

Leonardo was in a much more sombre mood. 'Anything?' he asked April.

'Not yet. They're going to repeat the interview at five o'clock and six o'clock. Maybe that'll help generate some new information.' She held up her fingers, crossed. 'We'll just have to wait and see.'

Leonardo gave a grunt. He was tired of waiting. On reflection, he'd realized that Raphael had a point. Maybe they should be trying to think of a way to track Splinter's kidnappers themselves.

April could see his concern. 'I told them to call me here *immediately* if anyone calls the studios,' she added reassuringly.

Leonardo looked up with a wan smile. 'Thanks, April. We really appreciate, you know . . . everything.'

'Hey, forget it.' She looked around, only now noticing that there were only three Turtles. 'Where's Raphael?'

The Turtles looked at one another. 'Uh, he went out,' said Donatello after a moment. 'Waiting here without any news made him feel cooped up. He needed to blow off some steam.'

'That's too bad,' said April. 'I was going to give you guys a tour of the antique store my dad left me.'

Leonardo shot a glance at the others. It was probably what they all needed, to get out from these four walls for a while. 'So, lead the way,' he said.

'It's not much really,' April explained as they went down the stairs. 'Just a junk shop, really. I can only afford to have somebody run it part-time. I do it mostly for my dad. He loved junk.' She gave a wistful laugh, and went on, half to herself: 'I guess it's silly to lose money on a business just because you miss your father . . .'

Donatello touched her arm. 'No, it's not.'

They had reached the bottom of the stairs. 'Are you ready?' said April, brightening out of her reflective mood. She threw open the door. 'Ta-daa!'

'Junk Shop' was certainly nearer the mark than 'antique store'. Not that that mattered to the entranced Turtles. They loved collecting junk – that was how they had come by all the possessions in their den, after all.

Donatello took a step forwards, entranced. He was staring at a stuffed and mounted polar bear rearing awesomely beside a carved mahogany bookcase. 'This place has got everything!' he breathed.

'Yup,' said April. 'Just about.'

Michaelangelo had found a pair of cymbals. Brandishing them wide apart, he crept up behind Leonardo's back with a mischievous grin on his face.

It was all Donatello and April could do not to burst out laughing as the cymbals swung together on Leonardo's ears. He gave a yelp of fright and leapt across the antique table in the middle of the room.

Then he turned and saw Michaelangelo holding the cymbals. '"Cymbal" things please "cymbal" minds,' he growled. 'Now, come here and let me show you how those things should *really* be played.' He advanced on Michaelangelo with a malevolent grin.

Michaelangelo was too doubled up with laughter to defend himself, and he was soon wrestled to the ground. 'Uncle!' he gasped between chuckles. 'I surrender.'

'What was that, bro'?' shouted Leonardo, pretending deafness. 'I can't *hear* you – I've got this *ringing* in my ears.'

'Uncle! Uncle, already!'

Leonardo gave Michaelangelo a playful cuff and then helped him up. They went on exploring the junk shop, larking around with various objects. Donatello, meanwhile, was engrossed in a stack of books that he had found.

For half an hour the three brothers were able to forget their woe. They left the shop in a somewhat more optimistic mood. Surely someone would see April's news report and phone in. Then, armed with a lead, they could set off to rescue their *sensei*. All four of them together.

April seemed to mirror their thoughts. 'Hasn't Raphael been gone a long time?' she asked as they returned to her apartment.

'Nah,' said Donatello. 'He's always doing it. He likes to go to a movie or work off some steam exercising on the rooftops. He'll pop back any time now.'

'And in a much better mood, I hope,' added Michaelangelo.

There was a tremendous crash as a window disintegrated into a hundred fragments. A green figure sailed through the air and landed heavily, rolling limply across the floor.

It was Raphael.

April screamed. She wasn't even sure if he was still alive.

15

'Raph!' cried Leonardo. He dropped to one knee beside the badly-beaten form.

April pressed a fist to her mouth in horror. She hardly dared to ask. 'Is he . . .?'

Leonardo touched his brother's neck, relieved to find a pulse. But it was dangerously faint. 'No, he's alive. Barely.' He looked up, his battle instincts kicking into action. 'Don, Mike,' he said urgently, 'cover the . . .'

It was too late. Multiple crashes splintered the air as every window in the apartment was broken in. Swarms of black-clad Foot ninja burst in. Some had shuriken or other exotic weapons, but most were armed with ninjato-swords. The setting sun glinted off the straight blades as they paced in around their prey.

'Whoa!' said Michaelangelo. 'And I thought

insurance salesmen were pushy.'

The three Turtles formed a circle to protect April and their wounded brother. The Foot moved nearer.

There was a metallic sigh as Leonardo's katana left its oiled sheath. Michaelangelo gritted his teeth and swung his nunchuku-flail, chopping the air like a rotor. Donatello swung his bo-staff into ready position, holding it poised like a javelin to thrust at any of the Foot ninja who came too close.

The trio presented a fearsome sight. Even a novice in the martial arts could discern, from their controlled movements and implacable focus, that they were masters of their weapons.

But they were outnumbered almost three to one. And, given reckless courage by their superior numbers, the first of The Foot shrieked battlecries as they ran in for the attack.

The first of them wielded a nunchuku. Seeing this, Michaelangelo grinned. 'Ahh, a fellow "chucker", eh?' He whipped the flail around his body in a show of dexterity. It made great *whoosh*ing sounds as it cleaved through the air.

The Foot stopped short. Their own nunchuku-wielder sniggered contemptuously and duplicated Michaelangelo's movements but with even more speed and force. He ended with one shaft of the flail tucked under his arm in the classic Bruce Lee posture, his show of intimidation complete.

Or so he thought. But he was rather taken aback when Michaelangelo's only response was to laugh.

The Turtle repeated his earlier display of skill, but this time holding nothing back. Now it was clear that he had barely been working up a sweat the first time. His technique completely outclassed The Foot champion's efforts. His flail swung up, down, right and left faster than the eye could follow, its motion making a single continuous swishing hum . . .

The Foot with the nunchuku gulped, and those next to him fell back a step. Suddenly Michaelangelo's nunchuku lashed out, felling him with a single crunching blow to the forehead.

'My advice is to keep practising,' remarked Michaelangelo to his unconscious foe.

By demonstrating his superiority, Michaelangelo had thrown the Foot warriors off-balance while giving the Turtles an advantage in morale. Donatello and Leonardo were quick to capitalize, launching themselves into the fray with gusto.

Donatello found himself facing a talkative Foot. 'I'm gonna turn you into turtle soup . . .' hissed the man.

'Oh, *man*,' replied Donatello, reacting with a wince. '"Turtle soup"? Are you kidding me? Like, I never heard *that* before, right? Where do you get your material?'

The Foot glared at him, eyes slitted behind the face mask. 'But first,' he said through gritted teeth, 'I'm gonna shell you like an oyster.'

Donatello shook his head disbelievingly. He showed his contempt for the blustering Foot ninja by turning to address Michaelangelo: 'Hey, bro', I got one here who's just begging for "the soprano maker".'

Michaelangelo took time off from clubbing an opponent of his own to glance over. 'Oh no, not "the soprano maker"!' he said in a high-pitched voice.

The Foot warrior had had enough. 'OK, hold still, lizard,' he said to Donatello, lunging forward.

Donatello raised his eyebrows – or would have, if he'd had any. '*Reptile*, please!' he corrected.

As the incensed Foot slashed down, Donatello casually dodged – but in doing so it seemed that his bo-staff slipped out of his hands. The Foot ninja, seeing his foe unarmed, raised his sword high for another attack.

But Donatello's apparent slip-up had a purpose. His bo had fallen over the leg of an upturned chair. Before the sword could descend, he stamped on the raised end of the bo – shooting the other end up with a painful thwack between his attacker's legs. The startled Foot gave an agonized yelp and toppled over, all the fight knocked out of him.

Donatello hooked the bo with his toe and flicked it up back into his hand. 'Try to think of it not so much as excruciating pain,' he said consolingly to the whimpering Foot, 'but more as your entrance fee into the Vienna Boys' Choir.'

Leonardo fought without wisecracks. 'Hey!' he called to his brothers as the three of them laid out more Foot ninja. 'Don't put all of these guys out – one of them must know where Splinter is.'

At that moment, a second wave of Foot warriors came pouring in through the broken windows. Now the intrepid Turtles were heavily outnumbered. 'I don't think that'll be a problem, Leo,' said Michaelangelo, grimacing.

The reinforcements turned the tide of battle in The Foot's favour. Leonardo was forced out to the upper landing of the stairway as he parried furiously against three combined attackers. As others followed, pressing their comrades on, Leonardo had no choice but to start retreating down the stairs.

The other two, meanwhile, were backed into a corner guarding April and the unconscious Raphael. Their swirling weapons flung the Foot warriors to and fro before they could get close enough to the Turtles to utilize their short ninjato.

Then a third wave of Foot warriors swung in through the windows. These were armed with bisento blades: massive long-handled battleaxes which gave them a long and lethal striking reach.

They closed in and swung at the two Turtles. Donatello and Michaelangelo ducked and wove, avoiding the powerful but ponderous blows which chopped great chunks out of the floorboards.

'Good thing these guys aren't lumberjacks,' commented Donatello.

Michaelangelo nodded as he backflipped out of the way of another swing. 'No joke!' he agreed. 'The only thing safe in the forest would be the *trees*.'

In the meantime, Leonardo had backed all the way down the stairs and into the junk shop. Here, the cramped space only allowed one Foot warrior to come at him at a time. As he battled on, there was the sound of hefty thuds from the apartment above and he noticed a shower of plaster falling down.

The apartment floor, weakened by the pounding it had taken from the bisentos, began to sag. At just the same moment, yet another wave of Foot ninja somersaulted in through the windows. Under their additional weight, the floor gave a splintering creak.

Donatello, quickly noting the extensive damage, yelled back to Michaelangelo and April, 'Brace yourselves, guys! I think —'

He didn't get any further. With a sickening crunch, the floor gave way and all of them – April and the Turtles as well as their sinister assailants – fell helplessly downwards.

16

Leonardo had noticed the shop ceiling buckling inwards in time to take shelter under an antique table. Many of the Foot ninja attacking him were not so lucky. He saw several of them struck by rubble or falling bodies, and one was hit on the shoulder by a chunk of timber.

Donatello and Michaelangelo landed agilely, helped by their ninjutsu training, but April struck the back of a chair with her midriff, which knocked the wind out of her. Raphael was fortunate to be out cold – landing limply did him no additional harm.

The lights snapped on. Standing in the shop doorway was Tatsu, arms folded arrogantly across his broad chest. His cruel mouth was set in a lopsided sneer.

Behind him were yet more Foot warriors. Completely fresh to the battle, they eagerly poured past their leader to encompass the beleaguered heroes.

April, recovering her breath after the fall, was just staggering to her feet. When she saw the predicament they were in, her shoulders slumped.

Tatsu held up his hand, palm outward. As it closed into a fist, the Foot ninja exploded into action.

Still extricating themselves from the debris, the Turtles were beset on all sides. They moved desperately to defend April and the still-senseless Raphael. Some of their attackers' blows began to break through their parries: Leonardo took a hefty whack from a nunchuku across the side of the head, a ninjato slashed Michaelangelo's forearm. The situation looked bleak indeed.

'Man,' gasped Michaelangelo, wincing from the pain of the wound he'd just taken, 'we could really use Raph right about now . . .!'

As if in answer to his prayers, a figure stepped out of the darkness and in front of a lamp. A long shadow was thrown across the scrummage of battling ninja.

Several of the Foot warriors sensed the newcomer's arrival and turned. Gradually the momentum of the fray subsided until everyone was staring at him. A tall, athletic figure in a hockey mask.

Casey drew a goalie's stick from his bag. 'You

guys mind telling me what you're doin' with my little green pal over there?' he demanded of The Foot. Then, noticing April, he added in jovial tones: 'Woo! An' who's the babe?'

April rolled her eyes. If they were going to be given a helping hand, did it have to come from a total chauvinist?

'Who the heck is *that*?' Leo said.

Michaelangelo shrugged. 'Wayne Gretsky, maybe? On steroids?'

Tatsu had heard enough. '*Yare!*' he commanded. 'Get them!'

Instantly the fight resumed, now with several Foot warriors detaching themselves from the attack on the Turtles to deal with Casey.

The situation was meat and drink to Casey. Merrily laying about him to left and right with the fearsome goalie's stick, he gave great whoops of childlike joy each time he connected with an opponent. 'Yeee-hah!' he shouted. 'It's *Hockey Night in Canada*!'

Heartened by the arrival of reinforcements – in however outlandish a guise – Leonardo and Michaelangelo were able to rally long enough to give Donatello cover as he hauled April and Raphael away from the heart of the mêlée.

Leonardo looked up to see a heavy bisento slicing through the air towards him. He ducked and the blade, passing over his head, tore into the wall. As the plaster crumbled, there was a shower of sparks – the bisento had sheared through

111

some electric cables. The Foot warrior wielding it jerked in a series of convulsive spasms and dropped in a heap. Simultaneously, the exposed cables sparked across the dry wood panels of the splintered wall.

The lights flickered out. Flames curled up along the wall, spreading rapidly through the junk-filled room.

As still more of The Foot entered from the stairwell, Leonardo called to the others: 'We've got to get out of here!'

They could see that the shop door and the stairwell were both secured by Foot warriors. It seemed to the Turtles that they were trapped. But then April began to drag Raphael's limp body behind some shelves at the back of the store.

The Turtles beat a retreat to find her pulling boxes away from the rear wall. A small half-door lay revealed.

'My grandfather used to sell more than junk during Prohibition,' explained April. 'There's an exit out to the street from his underground distillery.'

Leonardo nodded. He poked his head back into the store area to find the blaze raging from one end of the shop to the other. Casey was dealing savagely with a couple of Foot ninja who had lunged through a gap in the flames.

Another Foot had skirted the wall to attack Leonardo from the rear flank. He knocked him away with a reverse-stroke of his katana, motioning Michaelangelo and Donatello along the narrow opening between the shelves as he did so.

'We're getting out of here!' he yelled over the roar of the flames. 'You coming?'

Casey clubbed down a Foot warrior, chuckling manically. 'I'll cover ya!' he shouted back over his shoulder. As more Foot braved the inferno to race forward, Casey began a battling retreat towards the half-door.

As he reached it, the phone rang. Casey heard April's answering machine informing the caller that she wasn't at home. He took a last glance at the burning room. 'Babe,' he muttered under his breath, 'I don't even think you *got* a home any more . . .' And, from the sound of the caller's message that he could hear, she apparently didn't have a job any more either!

Casey turned to duck through the half-door. As he did so, a Foot ninja came charging around the shelves and drew back for a thrust at the vigilante's unguarded rear. Fortuitously, a blazing timber dropped from the roof and felled the man before he could strike.

Hearing the sound, Casey glanced back. 'That must have come as a blow,' he said as he closed the half-door and slid the bolt into place.

Hastily carrying their unconscious comrade through the cellar, the Turtles followed April to a low tunnel. They emerged through a trapdoor which gave on to the street.

Casey followed a few seconds later. The trapdoor was a tight fit for his muscular bulk. 'Phew!' he said, commenting on the reek in the cellar. 'Doncha just love the smell of cheap booze? Hey, babe – you do off licence sales?'

April ignored him. Running to her parked van, she started it up and let Casey slide behind the wheel while she helped the Turtles get Raphael into the back.

Sirens wailed along a street nearby. 'The cops,' muttered Casey. 'They'll sort those bozos out.'

Inside the burning building, Tatsu had the same thought. He looked up in annoyance as he heard the sirens. The Foot bisento-wielders had been on the point of hacking the cellar door open. He barked an order: 'Ninja, disperse. Vanish!'

From the back of the vw van, Donatello watched some of The Foot slipping off into the shadows. 'If we could follow them, they'd lead us to Splinter . . .' he reasoned.

Leonardo shook his head. He ached to find his master, too – but, in Splinter's absence, the mantle of responsibility had fallen on his shoulders. 'We have to get out of here,' he said. 'Somewhere way away – where we can tend to Raph and recover our strength.'

April nodded, numbly watching her shop and

apartment go up in flames. 'I know somewhere,' she said softly.

Casey gunned the engine and the van roared off down the street just seconds before a group of police cars arrived on the scene.

17

Later that night, at the warehouse that was the headquarters of The Foot, it was time for accounting.

The Shredder was not pleased. He listened to Tatsu's description of events with a cold swirl of fury rising in his black heart. Eyes narrowed to slits of icy hardness, he strode to where Splinter hung in chains and delivered a vicious backhand to the mutant rat's face.

'Who are these freaks?' he demanded. 'How have they learned to fight like this? *You – will – answer!*'

Splinter only raised his head slowly. He met the Shredder's gaze evenly, pausing for a moment before his mouth twitched into an unafraid smile.

This further enraged the Shredder, who delivered another mighty blow. Again Splinter could not be cowed. He gave the Shredder a level look as blood trickled down his snout.

With a choked-off gasp of thwarted fury, the armoured ninja lord turned on his heel and walked away. At the entrance of the chamber he came upon Tatsu. He stopped abruptly and glared at his lieutenant – the loss of face was the Shredder's, but the failure had been Tatsu's.

It was one of the harshest reprimands ever delivered by a superior, and all without a word spoken. Under the burning scrutiny of his lord's visored gaze, Tatsu was forced to swallow his pride. His eyes dropped to the floor.

The Shredder watched him a moment longer, radiating his displeasure, then stalked out.

Tatsu raised his eyes again. It was not penitence that filled them, but indignant fury. Why should he be blamed for the night's debacle? He had always served his lord loyally and with consummate skill! No, it was the ineptitude of the Foot warriors that had allowed the Turtles to escape. Standards had slipped since they moved to America and took to recruiting *gaijin* . . .

Tatsu stormed off in the opposite direction from the way his master had gone. As he went, he shoved crates angrily out of his path. He had been humiliated, and he was determined to find someone to pay for that.

In a piecemeal locker room in one corner of the

warehouse, many of the Foot warriors wounded in battle against the Turtles slumped exhausted on their benches. Tatsu entered in a blood-fury, rampaging around hurling objects against the locker doors. He began to berate the half-dressed ninja, blaming them for the mission's failure.

He lashed out at a young man who was too slow in getting out of his way. Nursing a split lip, the youth tried to slip away – but Tatsu, further enraged by his timidity, struck him again and again. 'Where is your *spirit*?' he snarled. 'Are you ninja, or are you docile sheep?'

Still the youth offered no resistance, and with each word Tatsu continued to pound him mercilessly. The anger had risen like a red tide in front of his eyes. He was uncontrollable.

But one youth suddenly ran forward out of the throng that were standing aghast at Tatsu's brutal show of force. It was Shinsho, who had been inducted as a full member of the Clan only the previous evening. He grabbed Tatsu from behind, pleading with him to stop beating his friend.

The bruised youth was cowering at Tatsu's feet. He stared up in horror as Shinsho caught hold of the senior ninja's arms. 'Shinsho!' he cried out. 'No . . .'

Instinct took over, momentarily replacing Tatsu's fury with the cold mechanical precision of the trained killer. An elbow to the ribs dislodged Shinsho's grip. Without looking, Tatsu immediately swung into a flying roundhouse kick that caught the hapless youth right on the side of his head.

Though crushingly hard, the kick in itself was not fatal. But when Shinsho was flung back, his head struck the floor with a deep crack. His flailing stopped abruptly in a last twitch of dying muscles.

The friend for whom he had intervened stumbled to his side. He searched in vain for a pulse. 'Shinsho . . .' he said in a desolate tone.

A group of younger recruits had by now gathered among the onlookers. They watched in shocked silence. They had been told that The Foot protected all its members – that it was more a family than a mere organization. Now they had witnessed the chief instructor slay a fully-fledged 'brother' for no better motive than simple annoyance. He had killed Shinsho as casually as another man might swat a fly.

His fit of spiteful anger now spent, Tatsu had a chance to reflect on his deed. He knew he had made a mistake. And his loss of control would serve only to disgrace him further in his master's eyes.

He gave a snort of disgust. There was nothing he could do about it now. He turned and walked off.

Danny Pennington would hear about Shinsho's death later. At the time that it happened, he was warily exploring an apparently-deserted corner of the warehouse. He had heard angry voices come from here, and had later seen Tatsu and the Shredder emerge from behind a grille.

Tatsu had left in such furious haste that the grille remained unlocked. Curiosity and trepidation warred inside Danny. At last he slipped from cover behind a crate and took a few faltering steps beyond the grille. He wanted to see what was so important that it had to be kept locked back here, and he was made more daring by the thought that both Tatsu and the Shredder had gone off to attend to other business elsewhere.

He found himself in a small dank room. He froze in amazement when he saw the dishevelled four-foot rat hanging in manacles on the opposite wall.

Splinter studied him serenely for a moment before speaking. 'How can a face so young wear so many burdens?'

Danny's mouth fell open. 'You . . . you can talk!' he managed to blurt out.

'Yes,' said Splinter. 'I can also listen.'

Danny's thoughts were in turmoil already. He had tried to help his new family, The Foot – and he had tried to show his loyalty to the Shredder – by telling them where to find the Teenage Mutant Ninja Turtles. But what had he accomplished? Scores of Foot warriors had limped home bruised and battered, the Turtles had escaped, and poor April's home had been burned to the ground.

121

Danny blamed himself. April had always been very nice to him, but all he'd done was steal from her and then betray her.

But how could he tell a talking rat all this?

'Some say that the path from inner turmoil begins with a friendly ear,' persisted Splinter. 'My ear is open, if you care to make use of it.'

Danny shook his head, confused. 'No . . . I – I don't think so . . .'

'What is your name?'

'Danny.'

'And have you no-one to go to, Danny? No parent? No guardian?' asked Splinter, his tone as calming as ever in spite of his debilitated state.

Danny guffawed. 'My dad couldn't care less about me,' he said resentfully.

Splinter slowly shook his head. 'I doubt if that is true.'

'Why?' demanded Danny, folding his arms.

Splinter's eyes filled with a wistful look. 'All fathers care for their sons . . .' he replied distantly.

Danny was annoyed. How could a giant rat know anything about his life? But then something occurred to him: if he really believed that, why then did he feel that Splinter's words struck a chord deep down? Maybe it was himself that he was actually annoyed with?

Hearing footsteps, Danny retreated to the grille. He took a last glance at Splinter, then he was gone.

18

The vw van reached its destination just after sunrise. By this time it was wheezing steam out of the bonnet, and April was glad to ease off on the pedal as they trundled the last half mile.

They had arrived at a ramshackle farm in upstate New York. It belonged to April's family and she had spent many happy summers of her childhood there. Now it was deserted most of the time, and the years had not been kind to the peeling paintwork and mildewed timbers.

All the same, April was glad to be there. Since her place in the city had burned down, this rickety old farmhouse was all the home she could lay claim to.

She stopped the van, clambered out and stretched her limbs in an extravagant yawn. 'Well,' she announced, 'this is it.'

Casey yawned and stumbled wearily down from the passenger seat. He had been pretending to sleep since April took over the driving from him some time after midnight. In reality, he'd kept one eye open most of the time – partly to keep an eye on April, who was well worth watching at any time, and partly to watch out for her driving. Casey had not fought off a horde of modern-day ninja just to get himself killed by a dozy female with no road sense.

He took a long hard look at the farmhouse. 'Nice,' he said in a tone that suggested quite the opposite. 'Didn't they use this place in *The Grapes of Wrath*?'

April turned to him with her mouth set in irritation. 'I told you I haven't been up here in years. Besides, all it needs is a little work . . .'

To belie her claim, one of the shutters chose that exact moment to swing out of place and fall with a clatter to the porch. Almost simultaneously, a sharp metallic bang could be heard from under the bonnet of the van – the kind of bang that spells serious trouble. Smoke billowed into the air.

Raphael had still not recovered consciousness. As the Turtles carried him upstairs, Casey distracted himself from his own thoughts of concern by taking a look under the bonnet of the van. Casey was a bit like Michaelangelo in that respect. When the serious cares of the world got too close, he preferred to think about something else. But at least Michaelangelo was prepared to face up to real relationships whereas, deep down behind his blustering façade, Casey was really afraid of getting close to another person.

But that April . . . mused Casey to himself. *Boy, I wouldn't mind getting real close to her.*

April came out of the farmhouse as Casey shut the bonnet. 'How is it?' she asked.

'Don't ask, toots. All I'll say is, you know any honest scrap merchants?'

April bristled. She was grateful to Casey for intervening in the battle with The Foot, but she couldn't see why he persisted in behaving like a nine-year-old. She started to reply in a voice dripping with irritation, but then she caught herself. It had been a long night, and they were all concerned about Raphael.

'Can you fix it?' she asked, forcing herself to sound polite.

Casey shook his head.

April sighed. 'Wonderful. Well, in that case I guess I've got a long walk ahead of me.'

'What for?' Casey slouched over to the porch and dropped into a rocking chair that nearly gave way under him.

'Our nearest neighbour's over four miles away,' said April, heading back inside. 'I need to get to a phone so I can let my boss know where I am.'

Casey got up and followed her through the door. 'Oh yeah, talking about phones . . . some guy named Charles called and left a message on

125

the answering machine before your place went up in flames.'

'What?' said April, turning to face him. 'Charles Pennington?'

Casey stroked the stubble on his jaw. 'Maybe. Is he the Charles that might say, for instance, "You're fired"?'

April stared at him aghast. Her mouth worked, but it was a few seconds before she got any sounds out of it. 'I'm . . . I'm *fired* . . .?' Suddenly she was fuming. 'What do you do, take *classes* in insensitivity?'

'Hey,' said Casey with a disinterested shrug, 'I was just trying to break it to you easy.'

'Well, you failed miserably.'

Casey levelled an admonishing finger at her. 'Look, "Broadzilla", you wouldn't even be standing here if it wasn't for me!'

'Oh.' April put her hands on her hips. 'So that's why you're following me around, is it? You're waiting for a "thank you".'

'Oh, *no*,' protested Casey sarcastically. 'It's me who should be thanking you for the sheer privilege of being here in your ancestral home!'

'Fine,' said April. She turned on her heel and stalked across the hall. '*Thank* you.'

'Thank *you*,' huffed Casey.

April paused in the doorway through to the living room. 'You're welcome!' she said through gritted teeth.

Casey was not about to let her have the last

126

word. He stormed over to the kitchen door. '*You're* welcome,' he said – then added, with a grin of gleeful malice: 'toots.'

The doors both slammed shut behind them as Donatello and Michaelangelo came down the stairs.

Donatello looked from one side of the hall to the other. Then he turned to his brother. 'It's kind of like *Moonlighting*, isn't it?' he remarked urbanely.

In the days that followed, each of the Turtles found his own way of dealing with the setbacks they had suffered. Not only were they wounded and dispirited after their battle with The Foot, but they had missed the chance to find out where Splinter was.

Raphael remained very ill – perhaps close to death. They could hardly begin to think how to treat him. The Turtles knew very little about healing skills beyond the rudiments of acupressure that Splinter had imparted to them. And they could hardly take their stricken brother to a doctor!

Instead they could only rely on instinct. Leonardo filled the bath half full and gently lowered Raphael into it stomach down. Raphael's shell had become soft to the touch. Leonardo wasn't sure if that meant he was beginning to recuperate, or if it indicated a turn for the worse. He pulled up a stool beside the bath and began a silent vigil. For days he refused to budge. April had to bring his food to him – and even then he seldom touched it. It was as though he was trying to pour all of his spirit into his unconscious brother. As though he was trying to will Raphael back to health.

The usually lighthearted Michaelangelo found that his own laid-back manner had quite deserted him. In his distress he became alone and withdrawn. He took to spending every waking moment in the barn, practising harder and harder at the death-dealing skills of ninjutsu. He fixed up an old duffel-bag to use as a punchbag, pummelling it mercilessly until the ferocity of his blows tore it apart. Then he directed his rage at a nearby sawhorse, splintering it with a single kick. He smashed axehandles and beams and wooden planks and anything else he saw lying around the barn. Finally he stopped, on the point of breaking through the barn door with his elbow strikes, because he noticed his vision had blurred.

He blinked, and realized he was crying.

Donatello latched on to Casey as a companion. He needed a carefree counterbalance to his naturally serious disposition. With Michaelangelo becoming more and more absorbed in his own introspection, Casey provided an acceptable substitute. The two of them worked together on fixing up a dilapidated old truck.

Casey tinkered around under the bonnet while

Donatello sat bored behind the wheel. They kept up a constant banter while they worked.

'No way,' Casey was saying as they argued about one of their favourite topics: old TV shows. 'Without a doubt it was the *Professor* and Maryanne that married. Happy ever after.'

Donatello shook his head. 'Not a chance, atomic mouth. *Gilligan* was her main man. Everyone knows that.'

'Bug off, barfaroni; Gilligan was a geek.'

'You're the geek, camel breath.'

'Dome head.'

'Elf lips.'

'OK,' said Casey, suddenly getting back to business, 'let's see if this has worked. Turn it over, fungoid.'

'All right, here goes . . .' Donatello hesitated. 'Uh, what're we on now?'

'G.'

'Oh, right,' said Donatello. '. . . Here goes, gack face.'

'I'm ready, hose brain.'

Donatello turned the key and the truck spluttered to life.

Before either of them could start to cheer, though, they realized that it was in gear. Casey had to dive out of the way as the van shot forwards and smashed halfway through the garage wall.

Dislodged shelves came crashing down around the truck as Donatello hastily switched off the engine. He stuck his head out of the window and smiled sheepishly at the startled Casey. 'It worked . . .' he began.

Casey flung a rag in his face. 'It sure did, *iota brain*.'

Suddenly there was a shout from the house that made them forget their squabbling. It was Leonardo's voice, and he was laughing in sheer joy.

'He's woken up!' he was yelling. 'Raphael's woken up!'

19

Leonardo had spent days alone in the bathroom keeping watch over Raphael. He had got so used to the anxious hush, broken only intermittently when the others looked in, that he found it a bit weird to find them all crowding into the room babbling excitedly.

Raphael was sitting up brightly in the bathtub. His shell was hard again. He looked fine, and he was asking for food.

The others joyously rushed off to prepare Raphael a true Turtle feast of deep dish pizza. Leonardo was left alone again with him for a short time. He gingerly laid a hand on his brother's arm.

'Listen, Raph . . .' he said. 'I've just been sitting here brooding about this all the time when it looked like you might not . . . well, you know. I wanted to tell you . . . about what I said that day about not needing you and all, I . . .'

In reply, Raphael reached up and put an arm round Leonardo's shoulders. He did not need to listen. He understood how Leo felt – how they both felt. They remained that way for a few moments, silently embracing, two brothers happily reunited.

April and Donatello arrived in the doorway. They had come to ask Raphael what toppings he wanted on his pizza. Moved by the scene that met their eyes, they stood in silence.

Donatello dabbed at a sentimental tear. 'It's a Kodak moment,' he said with a sniffle.

Leonardo and Raphael looked up at the sound, hastily disengaging from the hug and clearing their throats in embarrassment.

Aided by an enormous appetite, Raphael began to make a speedy return to full health. Even so, a lingering malaise still troubled the four mutant brothers. They still needed to know what had happened to their beloved master.

They threw themselves afresh into their training. Leonardo meditated and practised tag with deer in the woods nearby. It allowed him to sharpen his reflexes without harming anything. Donatello studied codes and tactics – other areas of the ninjutsu canon – and made new weapons for them all in the workshop. Michaelangelo returned to his hard exercises and martial *kata*, this time helping Raphael to recover the coordination and muscle tone he had lost while ill.

It did little good. Gnawing at them all of the time was their greatest dread, the thing that they could not face. The fear that, because of their failure, Splinter might be dead.

One afternoon soon after Raphael's recovery, Leonardo sat on a large log in the woods to meditate. Beside him was a deep pool covered with lilies. He stared into the wine-green water and cleared his mind of all distractions. There was still that last distraction, of course – that concern about Splinter's fate. But if he was to be true to his master's teachings, he must free himself of even that.

He recalled the words Splinter had spoken to him many times: 'You must concentrate only on the sitting, Leonardo; only on the *zazen*. Let go of everything else, and attain the state of no-mind . . .'

Leonardo was close to that state of *zazen*. He was thinking of Splinter, then his thoughts cleared. His mind became like a blank slate waiting for the touch of chalk, or like a pond moments before a stone is thrown in . . .

In a distant warehouse, Splinter looked up suddenly. 'Leonardo,' he whispered . . .

. . . And Leonardo saw him! His body straightened as if an electric shock had just run through it. He blinked. The image was fading now that his concentration was broken, but for a split-second it had been as though Master Splinter had touched Leonardo's mind with his own.

The next thing he knew, he was on his feet and racing back to the farmhouse, oblivious of the thickets of undergrowth and branches that he crashed through to get there.

The others looked up in surprise as he burst in.

'He's *alive*,' Leonardo gasped, breathless after his sprint. 'Splinter's alive!'

The other three looked at each other, puzzled and concerned. Donatello stepped forward and touched Leonardo's shoulder. 'We all think that, Leo,' he said. 'Of course he's alive. We *all* think he's alive . . .'

Leonardo refused to be humoured. He pushed Donatello's hand away forcefully. 'This is different, Don. I don't "think"; I *know*.'

There was something about the conviction with which he said this that registered with his brothers. They gave him a second look, and this time they recognized the utter certainty in his eyes.

That night, the Turtles went deep into the woods. As though driven by a force outside himself, Leonardo strode ahead like a sleepwalker, leading them until they arrived at a clearing. There they gathered twigs and branches in silence. It was not until the fire was lit and they all sat around in its orange-gold glow that anyone spoke.

Raphael was sceptical. He had heard Leonardo's story, but he found it hard to believe in mysticism. It was easier to accept that Leo's desperate hope that Splinter was alive had caused him to hallucinate.

'Leo,' he said, 'have you dragged us all the way out here just to sit around a campfire?'

'Don't worry, I came prepared,' interjected Donatello. He pulled out a bag of marshmallows.

Leonardo looked at him sternly. 'Put those away,' he said. 'Now, just do what I told you. Everybody close their eyes . . . clear your mind. Go beyond thinking.'

The others looked at one another, then at Leonardo. He had quickly resumed his traditional role as team leader. They shrugged and bowed their heads, meditating as he suggested.

A minute passed. Michaelangelo felt a mosquito settle on his face and wanted to scratch it away. He resisted the urge. In doing so, his mind passed beyond the concerns of the mundane world. He achieved another, higher, mental state. And, as he felt his brothers do the same . . .

. . . Splinter's translucent image appeared above the glimmer of the fire!

The Turtles gasped, but their eyes remained closed. The image of their master was not in front of them; it was inside their heads.

They heard his voice reaching to them across

hundreds of miles, and they listened awestruck. 'I am proud of you, my sons,' he said. 'Tonight you have learned the final and greatest secret of ninjutsu – that ultimate mastery is not of the body, but of the mind.'

None of the Turtles spoke. They hardly dared breathe, in case anything should disturb the entrancing state that had brought Splinter's image to them. He continued, his familiar calm wisdom restoring the fighting spirit they had lost since the Foot attack:

'Together, there is nothing the four of you cannot accomplish. Help each other. Draw upon one another . . .' The image started to fade, but they could still hear his words. '. . . And always remember the true force that bonds you. It is the same force that brought me here tonight. I return it gladly with my final words: I love you all, my sons . . .'

They opened their eyes as the last echoes of Splinter's voice diminished and got lost in the sighing of the night wind. Michaelangelo had only cried once before in his life – that day in the barn, when rage at his helplessness got the better of him. This time he shed tears unashamedly.

For a long time, until the moon set and the embers of the fire died away, the four brothers sat together in profound silence.

20

The following day, the Turtles began a totally new phase in their training.

Leonardo showed them how. 'We have to practise differently now,' he realized. 'When we're sparring, it shouldn't just be a question of trying to overpower each other. Remember what Splinter said.'

Michaelangelo was still breathing heavily after a strenuous practice bout against Raphael. He felt the workout had done them good. 'What else *is* sparring,' he objected, 'if you aren't trying to overpower the other guy?'

'Yeah,' agreed Raphael. 'Sheesh, pretty soon you're gonna start asking us to snatch pebbles from your hand, Leo.'

Leonardo went over to stand in the middle of the farmyard. He turned his mask around so that he was effectively blindfolded. Then drawing his katana, he assumed a ready stance.

'OK, now attack me,' he declared. 'All three of you at once.'

'Aw, come on, Leo,' said Raphael, folding his arms. 'What are you doing?'

Donatello shook his head. Maybe the strain of looking out for them all had finally proved too much for his big brother. 'You'll get hurt,' he warned Leonardo.

Leonardo heard their objections, but merely smiled. Suddenly he struck out with the katana, landing a stinging slap on Raphael's arm with the flat of the blade. 'Come on,' he said.

'Hey!' yelled Raphael, frowning. 'Knock it off, Leo. That hurt.'

'Come on, then,' said Leonardo again. He gave Raphael another whack.

Raphael rubbed his arm. 'Leo, I'm warning you . . .'

Leonardo just gave him a third slap, harder this time. 'Come *on*.'

Raphael was getting really steamed up by now. Since Leonardo's eyes were covered, he was obviously striking out blindly. That meant that he could easily inflict some real damage with the katana. Raphael had not struggled back to health only to have his crazy brother pigstick him with a sword while blindfolded. He decided to put a stop to this nonsense right away. Angrily drawing a sai, he leapt at Leonardo.

The katana struck out. Raphael's sai was dashed from his hand. It spun twice in the sunlight before coming to rest, point down, in the turf of a nearby field.

Raphael stood stunned. Surely it must have been a lucky blow . . . More cautious now, he drew his other sai and motioned for the others to join him. All three came at Leonardo in a tentative joint attack.

Three swings of the katana disarmed them all. Leonardo remained untouched. Although blind-folded, he seemed unassailable.

'*Rad*ical!' gasped Michaelangelo.

'*Eclec*tic!' ventured Donatello.

Leonardo pulled off the blindfold. He looked at Raphael, who still had not spoken.

Raphael spread his hands. 'Just call me "Grass-hopper" . . .' he said with a grin.

While the Turtles continued practising their new-found techniques, Casey and April were left to their own devices. At first they avoided one another as much as possible. Casey could not figure out why April got so irritated whenever he tried to act the gentleman. April, for her part, could not imagine how Casey got by in the modern world addressing women as 'chick' and 'sweetcakes'.

Gradually she warmed to him, though, realizing that Casey's crudeness was just a macho cover for a basically rather sensitive nature. One afternoon, when she entered the kitchen smeared with dirt after a stint of heavy labour, she found Casey manfully trying to cook up a stew for the evening meal. True, he was using Leonardo's katana to chop the vegetables, but at least he was making an effort. When, seeing her nursing a sore shoulder, he came over to give her a neck massage, April did not resist.

Later on, after dinner, she took Casey up to the attic and showed him various toys she had played with as a kid. She also brought out some sketches she had done since their arrival at the farm. Most showed the Turtles, but Casey was delighted to find one of himself in a propeller beanie. Flustered, April tried to yank it away. Casey firmly took it back and, after a moment of hesitation, he and April shared a laugh.

Meanwhile, the Turtles were increasing their understanding of ninjutsu by leaps and bounds.

Without Splinter to guide them, they had to invent training techniques of their own. Michaelangelo devised a game of 'ninja hot potato' in which an apple was tossed about, whoever caught it having to defend against the others in unarmed combat while taking a bite. Donatello tricked up a rotating shaft fitted with various poles of different lengths. Fitted up to a system of gears, it swung randomly and with great force, testing the user's reaction speed in blocking to the limit. Nonetheless, with their new understanding the Turtles had little trouble. They seemed to anticipate any attack exactly as it came. They had learned to respond instantly, entirely by instinct, without having to pause and think . . .

All except for Raphael. He had never fitted into the team quite so easily as the others. Also, he was uncomfortable with the idea of letting go of thinking. Deep down, Raphael was a bit afraid of his feelings – just as Casey had been. His introspective brooding had always helped him keep them at bay.

Now he had to get past all that. With his brothers' help, he trained hard using the blindfold. At first he just flailed about aimlessly, and the others easily penetrated his defence. Then he took to peeking, but he was soon caught out at this and prevented with jeers of 'foul!' and 'shame!'

At last, quite suddenly, he got it. His sais swished through the air, blocking the others' thrusts as though it was the most natural thing in the world to fight blind. Raphael could actually feel his instinct take over. He was ecstatic.

He lifted the blindfold, smiling broadly. They were all sweating and breathing heavily after the workout, but they were happy. They had attained the final lesson of ninjutsu.

Leonardo sheathed his katana with a click. Now they could rescue their master.

They found Casey and April sitting together on

141

the farmhouse porch to watch the sunset.

Casey gave a start. It always gave him a nasty turn the way the Turtles crept up out of nowhere. He could well understand why the ninja of old Japan had instilled such superstitious dread in their foes.

'Guys,' he complained, 'I told you I hate it when you do that . . .'

But April could see that the Turtles were not kidding around for once. 'What is it?' she asked.

Leonardo spoke for them all. 'It's time to go back,' he said simply.

21

For weeks there had been no challenge to the Shredder's supremacy. As his warehouse bustled with activity, he surveyed the whole of his operation from a lofty vantage point. The Foot scurried about below like his loyal ants, carrying in the stolen goods that enriched his hoard.

Another man might have been content, but the Shredder's posture was pensive. Inwardly he still burned with a cold fury that the Turtles had escaped. He knew that a wise man does not leave a single enemy alive.

Tatsu came and stood beside his master like a shadow, wearing the formal warrior's attire of kimono and stiff-winged *kataginu* overrobe. For all that he was a mighty ninja in his own right, he was in awe of the Shredder. He knew better than any man the Shredder's fierce pride and implacable drive. And he knew that he had yet to atone for letting the Turtles escape. It was that which weighed so heavily on the Shredder's mind.

At last Tatsu ventured to speak. 'Your empire flourishes, Oroku-sama,' he said.

The Shredder allowed a long interval to go by before he deigned to acknowledge Tatsu's presence. 'What news from the rat?' he said curtly.

'We have tried everything, lord, but still he will not speak.' After an uncertain pause, he continued: 'Why do they concern you so much, lord? They have not been seen in many days. They are gone from the city – perhaps for good . . .'

The Shredder did not turn when he answered. Instead he leaned on the rail and glared down like a hawk at the scurrying Foot below. 'When the Turtles were attacked . . . the way you recounted their fighting . . .' Behind his visor, the jewel-dark eyes narrowed; mostly to himself, he mused: 'Something familiar . . .'

It was raining as Casey steered the old truck back into the street above the Turtles' home. He pulled up where Leonardo directed and got out, shivering. He wished he had brought a jacket.

'What a homecoming, eh?' he remarked to April. 'This city . . .'

The Turtles did not mind at all. They were as at home in water as on land, so they enjoyed

144

the rain. Raphael stretched, working out a kink after being cramped up in the back of the truck for the long ride south. 'Now I know what it's like to travel without a green card,' he quipped.

Casey was looking over at the building next to where they had parked. 'So this is your place, huh?' he said. 'Y'know, it isn't too bad. Not bad at all . . .'

A metallic scraping sound echoed along the street. Casey turned to see Michaelangelo clambering into a manhole.

'You comin', dude?' said the Turtle.

As Casey realized where the Turtles really had their den, he dropped his head and sighed. He disliked confined spaces – particularly underground spaces, and even more particularly when they were awash with an unmentionable soup of muck, junk and slime. All the same, the Turtles were prepared to do it and he couldn't let them show him up in front of April. He followed them down.

The sewers were just as bad as he had imagined. The rainwater rushing down the centre of the tunnel carried soft glistening lumps that Casey did not care to inspect too closely. And the stench was appalling. He'd rather have taken on a dozen Foot any day. He held his nose and sloshed along with his shoulders hunched, glaring around in distaste.

'Great,' he grumbled. 'Just great. First it's

"The Farm That Time Forgot" and now this. Why don't I ever fall in with people who own *condos*?'

Donatello stopped at the den door. 'We're here,' he announced.

They swung the door open and stepped gingerly inside. The place was still in a shambles from The Foot's struggle to capture Splinter.

Casey was last through the door. 'I guess it's hard to get good maid service in a sewer,' he muttered.

April put her portfolio of sketches down on a table. 'Will you quit complaining? It's just for one night.'

Raphael was impatient for action. 'I still don't see why we don't just get started right away,' he griped.

'Raph, it's been a long drive,' Leonardo reminded him. 'Before we go out and announce to The Foot that we're back, we could all use a few hours' sleep.'

Raphael nodded. 'Yeah, I know. You're right. It's just that I'm anxious to —'

A bump from one of the cupboards interrupted him. Instantly alert, the Turtles brought out their weapons and inched warily closer. Donatello and Michaelangelo moved to the side and, each taking a handle, waited for Leonardo's signal to pull the cupboard doors open.

Raphael saw an arm, reached in, and pulled the interloper past them into the room. At the same moment, Leonardo drew his katana back, ready to thrust down in a split-second.

Then they all relaxed. It was only Charles Pennington's son.

'*Danny?*' said April, astonished.

Danny cowered with his hands over his head. 'D-don't shoot!' he cried.

Raphael shot a wry glance at Leonardo's sword, which was still poised above the boy's head. 'I don't think it's loaded, kid,' he teased.

Danny took a peek up between his fingers. Seeing Leonardo sheath the katana, he found the courage to get to his feet. But he remained tense and frightened.

April came over to him. 'Danny, what're you doing here?'

Danny didn't know what to say. He knew that this hideout was where the Shredder's ninja had apprehended Splinter, but he could not bring himself to tell April about his involvement with The Foot. Then she would realize that it was he who had betrayed her. 'Well,' he blurted, 'I . . . I . . . ran away from home.'

'Oh, God!' said April. 'Your father must be having kittens!' She headed over to the phone. 'Does this thing work?' she asked Donatello.

Danny rushed over to stop her. 'No! Please . . . don't call him. Just let me stay here the night with you. Please? We can call him in the morning, I promise.'

April chewed her lip. 'Well . . .'

'Hold it! Hold it!' said Casey. He had just taken in what April had said to him as they entered the den. 'What's all this about spending the night down here . . .?'

Donatello guessed the truth. 'Casey, you're a claustrophobe!'

Casey had never got much beyond the eighth grade. 'Hey, you want a fist in the mouth?' he demanded, pointing at Donatello. 'I'm strictly a ladies' man, OK?'

April tried not to laugh. 'Don meant that you're afraid of enclosed spaces,' she explained.

Casey switched to the defensive. 'Afraid? Me? Is that what you think?' he said, bristling with feigned indignation. 'Well, hey, I don't have to take this stuff about bein' *afraid*. I'm gonna go sleep in the truck!'

Great, he was thinking; that gets me out of having to spend the night in this rat-hole.

But he did not fool April. As he stormed out, she couldn't help dissolving into a fit of giggles.

Danny, meanwhile, had found her sketches of the Turtles. 'Wow, these are really excellent,' he enthused.

'Thank you.' April was flattered. She had a minor in Art, but her job gave her few chances to make any use of it these days. Scratch that – it *had* done. For a moment she'd forgotten that she did not actually have a job any more.

Danny picked out a drawing of Michaelangelo swinging his nunchukus. 'You think maybe I could

148

have one?' he said as he admired it.

April hesitated.

'Please?' he said. 'Just so I'll know all this really happened.'

'Well, OK . . .' April relented. 'Sure. Why not?'

'Good choice, kid,' said Michaelangelo, looking over Danny's shoulder as he passed by. He rubbed his stomach. 'Boy, I could really go for a little deep dish action right about now.'

'I brought a pizza down here the other day,' said Danny. 'There might be some left over.'

He pointed to a pizza carton on the table near Donatello. Michaelangelo shot across the room like an eager bloodhound, but not before Donatello had picked up the carton and looked inside it.

'Well?' said Michaelangelo, his mouth watering in anticipation.

Donatello held up a finger. 'A question.'

Michaelangelo nodded. 'Yeah? What?'

'Do you like penicilium on your pizza?'

He showed the contents of the carton to Michaelangelo, who grimaced in disgust.

Donatello ambled off humming Tchaikovsky's *Funeral March* and dropped the carton into the waste bin. 'Maybe we can pick up a takeaway for breakfast,' he said.

22

Casey, asleep in the front of the truck, later that night, was suddenly woken by the sound of a manhole cover clanking on wet tarmac. He twisted uncomfortably on the seat and looked out.

The street lamp illuminated a figure emerging from the sewers. It was Danny Pennington. After glancing around and satisfying himself there was no-one in sight, he replaced the manhole cover and loped off down the street.

Casey couldn't sleep anyway. He kept getting the gear stick in his back, and the steering wheel made a poor substitute for a pillow. Stretching, he clambered out of the truck and ran swiftly and silently after the boy.

It was not difficult for Casey to keep up. He was a lot fitter than Danny, who occasionally smoked a furtive cigarette when his father was not around. Eventually they came to a bridge. Danny hurried across, still shadowed by Casey.

The Shredder's warehouse was on the other side. At this time of night most of the activity inside had died down. There were a few lights on, but most of the recruits had been asleep for hours. Danny paused outside the door to tie a band around his head. Then he slipped inside.

Casey darted across to the door, listened for a moment, and pushed it open. He was staggered by the extent of what he saw inside. There was enough contraband to fill fifty stores.

The approach of a couple of Foot sentries jerked him back to the immediacy of the situation. He retreated behind a crate to avoid being seen. By the time the sentries were safely past, however, Danny was nowhere in sight.

Casey set out to pick up his trail again, but he soon got fed up with having to duck out of sight every time he heard someone coming. To remedy the situation, he ambushed a hooded Foot ninja between a row of packing crates and laid him out with a hefty punch. Pulling the limp form out of sight, Casey hastily stripped off the Foot's *dogi* and put it on over his own clothes. It was a tight fit, but it would do the trick. Now he could move around the warehouse unhindered.

Casey pulled the mask down over his face, covering a grin of childlike pleasure. Oh boy, was he going to kick some ass . . .

*   *   *

Danny found himself wandering to the back of the warehouse, to the place where Splinter was held prisoner. He looked inside, relieved that the gentle rat was still there. He dreaded coming back one day and finding the chains hanging empty, but he knew that Tatsu or the Shredder would eventually kill Splinter. Danny would miss him then. Splinter was the only one to have shown him any real kindness during his stay at the warehouse.

Splinter raised his head slowly. When he spoke, his voice was very weak. 'I have not seen you in many days.'

Danny shuffled his feet. 'I've been at my hideout a lot lately.'

Splinter raised his eyebrows. 'And do you now hide from your surrogate family as well?' he asked.

Danny heaved a long sigh. 'I don't know . . .'

'I, too, once had a family, Daniel.'

Danny looked up. Everything Splinter said sounded so wise, as if he had all the answers – as long as you were prepared to listen. Danny suddenly found that he was willing to listen.

'Many years ago,' Splinter told him, 'I lived in Japan, a pet of Master Yoshi. Then I was but a normal rat, for this was years before I was exposed to the mutagen that made me as I am now. My cage was in the *dojo* where Yoshi spent

153

each day in practice, and I mimicked his movements as he performed the *kata*. Thus I learned the mysterious art of ninjutsu, for Yoshi was one of the finest shadow warriors of his clan.

'Yoshi's only rival was a man named Oroku Nagi, and they competed in all things – but in no matter more fiercely than over the woman they both loved, a beautiful woman named Tang Shen.'

Danny listened intently. Already it seemed inevitable how the story would end – Splinter's tones were laced with tragedy. The rat continued: 'One night, Tang Shen confessed to Oroku that she did not reciprocate his feelings. She loved only my master. Oroku flew into a violent rage and began to beat her viciously. He might have killed her, but then Yoshi arrived. The two men fought, and in the struggle Oroku was killed . . .'

Danny moved closer, wide-eyed with fascination. The story was not turning out as he had expected at all.

'The clan's code of honour was clear,' went on Splinter, 'Yoshi should have performed *seppuku* – ritual suicide. But he chose to place love above honour. Instead, he took Tang Shen and me with him to a new life here in America.'

Danny waited expectantly. If they had fled from the clan's vengeance, what then had happened to Yoshi and Tang Shen?

Splinter was about to tell him: 'Oroku Nagi left behind a younger brother, Oroku Saki. He was six when my master left Japan, but he swore then that he would exact vengeance for his brother's death. He trained hard, fuelling his spirit with hatred, and he grew to become the most feared ninja warrior in all the Orient. Honing his skills with acts of thievery and violence, finally he was ready to pursue Yoshi to New York and here fulfil his vow.'

Splinter's voice dropped to an appalled whisper: 'I remember the night well, every detail indelibly etched on my memory, as my master returned home to find his beloved Tang Shen lying lifeless on the floor. Her killer was still in the apartment, stalking up to him from behind, and I went frantic in my cage trying to give a warning. Then Yoshi turned, just as Oroku Saki fell upon him with drawn sword . . .

'My cage was broken in the battle, and I leapt at Oroku's face, biting and clawing. But he threw me to the floor and took one slice with his katana. His blow took off half my right ear; if I had been any slower, it would have taken my life.

'Then he was gone, and I saw that my desperate attack had come too late to save my master. He lay inert across his beloved Tang Shen, his lifeblood spreading in a widening pool. I was alone.'

Danny stared at Splinter. The rat's obvious profound sadness was so palpable that for a moment he could not speak. Finally he asked, 'What happened to this "Oroku Saki"?'

'No-one really knows . . .' Splinter looked into Danny's eyes, then lifted his gaze to the dragon-crested headband. '. . . But you wear his emblem on your brow.'

Danny's fingers went up to the headband. A look of horror spread across his face as he made the connection. Oroku Saki was the Shredder . . .

The realization decided him. He had finally made up his mind where he stood. He had got in deep with these thugs and criminals, but it was not too late to back out. He untied the headband and let it drop to the floor, his lip curling in dis-taste at the sight of the hated Foot emblem.

Then his expression turned to one of sick terror as a familiar voice rang out through the room:

'What are you doing in here, boy?'

It was the Shredder —!

23

Danny whipped around, his face draining of colour. He wanted to run, but he was so terrified that he had no strength at all. He stood quivering like a rabbit as the armoured ninja lord strode imperiously towards him. Tatsu followed close behind his master.

The Shredder stood right in front of Danny. But his gaze was directed over the boy's head, at the far wall where Splinter hung. 'I asked you a question,' he said.

Danny struggled to get a grip on himself, even though every nerve in his body just wanted to curl up into a ball and hide. 'N-nothing . . .' he managed to stammer.

The Shredder looked down at him now. His eyes had no trace of human mercy in them. 'You're lying to me,' he stated.

Danny flinched. 'No . . .'

The Shredder scrutinized him like a snake watching a mouse. 'And you're hiding something from me,' he said. He extended a gauntleted hand over Danny's head. Without his eyes leaving the boy's, he began to trace around the outline of his body. It was as though his hand was a kind of metal detector, probing an invisible field. Danny squirmed, growing more and more nervous.

The Shredder's hand stopped next to Danny's jacket pocket. He reached in and extracted a piece of paper, which he unfolded with menacing slowness. It was the sketch that April had done of Michaelangelo.

The Shredder studied the picture for a few seconds, darkly contemplative. He turned to Tatsu. 'They're back,' he said simply.

The dull peal of the alarm roused The Foot to full alert. Within minutes the warehouse had become a hive of bustling activity, as an entire army of black-hooded ninja amassed in the assembly area.

On the way to make a pre-battle inspection of his troops, the Shredder issued his commands to Tatsu. 'There will be no mistakes this time. I go myself.'

Tatsu lowered his head slightly, chagrined. He had still not recovered his master's full confidence since the last debacle.

'Tatsu. The rat . . .'

Tatsu looked up, waiting expectantly to see how he could serve.

'. . . Kill it,' said the Shredder.

Danny had heard everything. As the Shredder marched out at the head of his ninja horde, he ran back to the room where Splinter was confined. As yet he had no plan to get the rat free. He needed help – but from where? Here in The Foot headquarters, he was surrounded by enemies.

One of the ninja stragglers suddenly grabbed him and manhandled him behind a stack of boxes.

'Hey . . .' said Danny, struggling. 'Hey! What're you doing? What . . .'

Several other stragglers hurried by. The one who had seized Danny held up a finger to shush him.

Danny was puzzled. 'Who are you . . .?' he asked hesitantly.

Casey yanked off the hood of his borrowed *dogi*. 'Recognize me now, kid?' he snapped. 'And you've got one hell of a lot of explaining to do, you little —'

Danny recognized him, all right. For all Casey's grumpiness and bluster, he knew him as one of the good guys. It seemed his prayers had been answered. 'You've gotta come with me!' he said.

'What are you talkin' about, come with you?' snorted Casey. 'In about two seconds I'm gonna punch your lights, you slippery little brat.'

'They're gonna kill *Splinter*!' protested Danny.

Casey eyed him dubiously. Trust did not come easily to someone of Casey's suspicious nature at the best of times, and Danny had certainly done nothing to demonstrate his sincerity.

'All right,' he decided, shoving Danny ahead of him. 'But if you're up to something . . .' He showed Danny his big fist.

The pair of them darted quickly across the nearly-deserted warehouse, to the secluded area at the back where the Shredder's prisoner was manacled. Splinter looked up weakly as they came in.

Casey had learned from April that the Turtles' ninjutsu teacher was a giant rat, but hearing her account and confronting the reality were two different matters. More than a little taken aback by the sight, he nonetheless stepped quickly over to inspect the manacles.

'Who are you?' said Splinter.

Casey ignored the question at first. Turning to Danny, he called back, 'Where do they . . .?'

Danny, anticipating the question, tossed him a set of keys from a hook by the entrance.

As Casey unlocked the chains, he told Splinter how he came to be there: 'I'm Casey Jones. I'm . . .' He paused in mid-sentence, realizing he was about to use words that he had not spoken in a very long time. '. . . I'm a friend.'

As the last manacle was removed, Splinter slumped forward into Casey's arms. He gritted his teeth against the pain of returning circulation and the cramp in long-inactive muscles.

Danny came over to help, and together they helped Splinter limp towards the entrance.

'OK,' said Casey, 'let's get the hell *out* of here.'

A shadow fell across the entrance, arms folded defiantly across a broad chest. It was Tatsu, a cruel smile spreading across his heavy-jowled face. And behind him surged a mob of recruits.

A few of the older thugs began to move in, but Tatsu held them back with an angry grunt. He wanted the pleasure of despatching the rat and his friends by himself.

Casey pushed Splinter and Danny behind him. He dropped into a half-hearted boxing crouch as he watched Tatsu come in towards him. For such a big man, Tatsu was light on his feet. Casey knew he had a hard fight ahead.

Tatsu's fist lashed out, snapping Casey's head back. He reeled, arms flailing, and staggered back into a pile of stolen goods. Still half-stunned, he twisted his feet under him and forced himself up as Tatsu closed in.

'Lucky punch,' said Casey, spitting out a tooth. 'You're gonna *pay* for that dental work, Tinkerbell . . .'

Tatsu slammed a reverse roundhouse kick into his jaw. Casey went spinning back and crashed into a crate of contraband.

161

He got to his feet groggily. 'I don't think you're listening . . .' he said through swollen lips.

Tatsu took a rapid sidestep forwards, doubled his opponent up with a forearm smash, then delivered a knee to the chin that sent him flying backwards.

Casey slammed into the corner and reeled about from wall to wall, staying on his feet more by luck than anything. 'I'm . . . really startin' to pick up on a little communication problem here . . .' he gasped, dabbing groggily away at a stream of blood coming from his nose.

Tatsu laid into Casey mercilessly. Just as he staggered back from one punishing kick or punch, another landed that sent him crashing across the room. Tatsu never gave his opponent time to recover. He used Casey like a punch bag, pummelling him with blow after blow until his face and body were a mass of bruises and cuts.

Finally Casey slumped down on to yet another pile of stolen goods. He tried to get up, but all he managed was a dazed groan. Painfully he opened his eyes. What he saw gave him a faint ray of hope, for he had come to rest on a heap of sports goods and right under his arm was a golf bag.

As Tatsu approached, Casey slowly removed a golf club from the bag.

Tatsu stood over him. His lips were twisted in a lopsided sneer as he contemplated the *coup de grâce*. He raised his foot ready to stamp down on Casey's spine. 'Farewell, *gaijin*,' he hissed.

Casey drew on his last reserves of strength. Despite the agony in every muscle of his battered body, he twisted round and drove the head of the club into Tatsu's stomach.

Tatsu grunted in pain and surprise and doubled up. Casey struggled to his feet, planted himself for a big tee shot, and swung. 'Fore!' he yelled like a *ki-ai* shout. The club struck Tatsu right on the point of the chin, actually lifting him off the ground before his body crashed down on the floor. There he lay, spreadeagled and out cold.

Casey kissed the club. 'I'll never call golf a dull game again.'

A movement reminded him of the recruits who had entered with Tatsu. He turned to face them, still shaky on his feet after the pounding he had taken. Still, he would give them a good fight. Now he had a weapon.

But the recruits were not so sure they wanted a fight. Most of them were milling around in confusion, and some actually seemed pleased that Tatsu had fallen.

Not so the older thugs. One – the leader of the youths who had set upon April in the car park – growled at the others to back him up. 'Well, why are we just standing here? Let's get him!'

Casey hefted the club. 'You gonna be first, junior?' he said thickly.

The youth hesitated. Casey was wounded and dazed, after all, but he had managed to floor Tatsu. 'He can't stop us all!' he snarled.

No-one moved.

'Look what he did to *sensei* Tatsu!' declared the youth angrily.

'Tatsu!' put in Danny scornfully. 'He killed Shinsho.'

There was a murmur from the other kids. That got home to them more deeply than anything that had been said so far.

The head youth was not ready to back down. 'That was an accident!' he snapped. Still no-one moved. He played his trump card: 'We took an oath of loyalty. The Shredder is our *master*.'

Splinter had been recovering his strength. Now he spoke, and the teenagers were as rocked by his clear, level tones as much as by the sight of a talking rat.

'The Shredder *uses* you,' he informed them. 'He poisons your minds to obtain that which *he* desires. He cares nothing for you, or for the people you hurt. Forget your oath of loyalty; there is no dishonour in turning against an evil master.'

The rest of the group were affected by Splinter's words, but still the head thug refused to give up. He had not forgotten that when he was in prison, it was the Shredder who had him bailed out. 'We're a *family*!' he cried.

'A family?' said Casey. 'A *family*?' He made a fierce sweeping gesture that included the contraband-stuffed warehouse, Tatsu, and the prison where Splinter had been chained. 'Is this the kind of "family" you really want?'

Casey moved over and gently put Splinter's arm on his. It was debatable which of them was in the worse condition. Slowly they helped one another limp over to the entrance, with Danny bringing up the rear. The doorway was still blocked by a group of teenagers. Casey and Splinter stopped and waited.

A moment went by. Then the group dispersed to let them go through.

24

The Foot warriors moved like shadows through the streets, all but invisible even to the cats that skulked along the alleyways by night. The Shredder loped along at their head, his spiked metal armour doing nothing to diminish his tiger-like stealth. Under the blank faceplate, his nostrils flared. He could almost smell the blood of his foes on the sweet night air. Soon they would lie dead at his feet, perishing as did all who opposed the supremacy of Oroku Saki – the Shredder.

When his troops reached the manhole cover above the Turtles' lair, the Shredder stood aside and watched his ninja pour through like a torrent of inky darkness.

'Night's black agents to their preys do rouse . . .' he muttered with malefic glee. Then he, too, slipped silently through the manhole and into the den of his foes.

The first of The Foot paused as they reached the Turtles' boarded-up doorway. Should they wait for the Shredder to arrive? Communicating by means of the *kuji kiri* – secret finger signals known only to the exponents of ninjutsu – they reached a decision: invade now, so that they might gain the glory of capturing the freaks for their master.

A powerful kick reduced the door to broken planks. The first group of ninja rushed forward, but their bloodlust dissolved into milling confusion as they saw that the room was empty.

They crept tentatively further into the den. There was every sign that the place had been occupied quite recently, but now it was quite deserted. A few of the ninja glanced at one another and shrugged. One of them relaxed from his posture of wary tension and scratched his head in puzzlement.

Suddenly a blast of steam billowed down from the pipes overhead. Flinching, the Foot invaders stared up to see a quartet of agile green shapes leaping down towards them. The next instant they were beset by punches, kicks and weapon-strikes seeming to come at them from every direction out of the steam. Taken utterly by surprise, they were soon overwhelmed.

Raphael shut off the valve to the pipes. As

the steam melted away, the Turtles found themselves standing amid a crumpled heap of some two dozen Foot warriors, their groaning bodies draped all around the room.

Raphael tossed away an apple that he had been eating during the fight. 'Gee, guys, I'm not sure about the sauna attachment,' he said nonchalantly. 'What do *you* think?'

'I just hope there's more of them,' said Michaelangelo, smirking at the vanquished ninja.

He got his wish. As he spoke, a second wave of Foot warriors came darting through the shattered door.

The Turtles no longer had the advantage of surprise, but they could counter the attackers' superior numbers by their own use of strategy. They had moved the furniture so that only a small group of Foot could actually get into the fray at any one time.

More *dogi*-clad bodies soon piled up around the den. The Turtles had yet to work up a sweat.

Michaelangelo decided to make things a bit more interesting for himself. He picked on one ninja in particular, guiding him to a specific spot in the middle of the room with a series of harassing blows from his nunchuku.

'A little more to the left . . .' he said, giving the Foot a whack on the side. 'And a little more . . .' Another tap. 'Right there. Stop. Perfect.'

The Foot was enraged, but Michaelangelo's

blows had not been hard so he remained unhurt. Glaring at the grinning Turtle, he snarled, 'Mock me, eh? Well here's where you get turned into mock turtle soup, freak!'

'There's obviously just the one Foot joke book,' remarked Michaelangelo casually as a bo-staff suddenly stabbed down from the ceiling and knocked the angry Foot warrior senseless. He dropped in his tracks without knowing what hit him.

Michaelangelo looked up to the open ventilation grate where April was sequestered with staff in hand. 'You're a natural, sis,' he said, giving her an OK sign.

'Why, thank you,' said April, beaming. 'Want to steer another one over here for me?'

Michaelangelo spotted another Foot warrior racing towards him and grinned. 'Coming right up!'

Unable to deploy their superior numbers, the Foot were soon forced back to the entrance. As they stumbled back into the ranks already crowding the dank tunnel, there was a cry of 'Gangway!' and Donatello came cannoning along on his skateboard, skilfully swishing his bo like a scythe as he went. Foot went flying like ninepins ahead of him.

'Yee-hah!' whooped Donatello, swinging the skateboard on the spot as he littered the tunnel with desperately retreating Foot.

'Show-off,' Raphael shouted after him.

'Come along,' called Leonardo, racing along the tunnel behind Donatello. 'We've got them on the run now.'

At the back of his warriors, the Shredder looked on with distaste. He could not see precisely what was going on, but he could tell from the cries echoing along the tunnel and from the disordered ranks ahead of him that his Foot warriors were losing the battle. Somehow the Turtles had sensed the sneak attack before it came.

The Shredder glanced up at the open manhole. Obviously the Turtles would press their advantage, carrying the battle all the way back to the street. Such was the impetuosity of youth! Well, let them come. Once out of their lair, they would soon fall to his superiority. He launched himself in a powerful leap and swung up into the street. Had there been anyone nearby at that hour, they would have seen no more than a fleeting blur of motion. Within seconds, the Shredder had melted away into the shadows like a ghost.

The Foot warriors left the sewer altogether less gracefully, propelled by their panic-stricken flight from the Turtles. Once up in the open air, they tried to regroup and launch a fresh assault, but the Turtles' new fighting skills were more than a match for them. Donatello shot up out of a storm drain cover and rolled fluidly into a bunch of Foot, bowling them down. He was on his feet in a trice, and his staff swung back to scatter the ninja as they tried to rise.

The Turtles fought on almost frivolously, the uncanny sixth sense they had developed in the last phase of their training giving them an overwhelming advantage. Soon fallen Foot warriors littered the street.

Michaelangelo floored a couple with a spinning kick, then looked around for fresh opponents. Nearby, Leonardo and Raphael were chasing a few disorderly stragglers up a fire escape.

'Hey! Wait for me!' yelled Michaelangelo.

Momentarily distracted, he failed to notice the Foot who had been playing possum right behind him. Seeing the Turtle with his back turned, the Foot silently rose and drew back his ninjato to strike without warning. The blade flashed in a deadly arc towards Michaelangelo's neck. But the treacherous swordsman had reckoned without the Turtles' newfound combat intuition. At the last instant, Michaelangelo pulled his head down into his shell so that the blade sliced harmlessly through empty air.

Michaelangelo popped his head back up and half turned. 'Sneaky,' he commented, lashing back with a forearm strike that knocked the swordsman cold. Filled with exuberation, Michaelangelo punched towards the heavens. 'I *love* being a Turtle!' he yelled.

The Foot had retreated as far as the rooftop. There was nowhere else to go. As they milled about in search of an escape route, the four Turtles arrived at the top of the fire escape. The two groups squared off against each other. The Turtles grinned as they saw their demoralized foes hesitate. They were on the verge of total victory —

Suddenly, from a higher rooftop, a shadowy figure launched itself down between the opposing groups. As the Foot ninja peeled back, the Turtles laid eyes on their chief foe at long last. The Shredder was joining the fray.

25

The Shredder stepped forward in silence. Moonlight gleamed off his blade-covered armour. He raised his gauntlets to display their serried knives.

'Anybody have any idea who this is?' Leonardo asked his brothers.

'I dunno . . .' said Michaelangelo, 'but I bet he never has to look for a can opener.'

The ninja lord spoke: 'You fight well, in the old style, but you've caused me enough trouble. Now you face the Shredder.'

Donatello looked at the others quizzically. '"The Shredder"?'

Michaelangelo shrugged. 'Maybe all that hardware's for makin' coleslaw.'

The Shredder reached out his hand. One of the Foot behind him tossed him a six-foot-long bo.

175

He twirled it in a display of martial elegance, then set himself for battle.

'I got him,' announced Raphael confidently. He leapt at the Shredder with both sai-daggers. The staff swung round, catching Raphael and sending him flying back to land flat on his shell, more surprised than hurt.

'Oh-oh,' said Michaelangelo. He did not like the idea of a foe who was good enough to simply toy with them.

Leonardo went in next – more warily, after he had seen the ease with which the Shredder handled Raphael. He fared no better. A double swipe with the shaft of the bo sent him reeling.

Donatello and Michaelangelo looked at each other. One of them would have to try next, even though there didn't seem much hope. They had never faced an opponent so skilled in ninjutsu before.

'Flip you for it?' suggested Michaelangelo.

They each rushed the Shredder in turn – only to be flung back as effortlessly as the other two had been.

Meanwhile, Casey had arrived on the scene with Danny and Splinter. The aged rat master of ninjutsu was now walking unaided. Casey admired his stamina – or perhaps it was sheer force of will that kept him on his feet. After his weeks of deprivation, Splinter should have been barely able to crawl, but he was driven by anxiety about the fate of his pupils.

176

April, streaked with dirt from the ventilation duct, squirmed up out of the manhole to join them. She was astonished to see the area strewn with dozens of unconscious Foot warriors. For a few seconds she thought the Turtles had already won. Then, seeing where the others were looking, she turned her gaze up to the roof and her jubilation turned to anguish. The Shredder was striking out again and again, badly clobbering the Turtles.

Casey would have liked to get up there and lend a hand, but his body was a mass of aching bruises after the run-in with Tatsu. He could barely hobble along. He shook his head and turned to make a comment to Splinter: 'Looks like your boys are taking a pasting . . .'

Casey stopped and looked around in bewilderment. Splinter had slipped away without a sound. Now he was nowhere in sight.

Then Casey spotted several Foot ninja gathering on the pavement under the fire escape. They were preparing to climb up to the roof and aid their master. Casey didn't think the Shredder looked as though he needed any help – and the Turtles certainly didn't need any more trouble. But he was hardly in any shape to intervene . . .

Then his gaze wandered to a garbage truck parked nearby. It had been abandoned by its driver at the outbreak of the fracas. Casey limped over and got into the cab, threw the truck into gear, and accelerated towards the fire escape.

The Foot had already started climbing. Casey took the truck up on to the pavement and ploughed right on through the fire escape. It buckled and gave way higher up, bringing the ninja showering down in a tangle of flailing limbs and twisted metal.

On the roof, the Turtles were regrouping and trying to formulate some kind of tactics. 'OK, guys,' said Leonardo, breathing heavily, 'let's apply a bit of teamwork here.' They all rushed in together, but to no avail. The Shredder dodged their attacks with ease, hardly bothering to move at all as he swung his weapon with the same pinpoint accuracy.

Michaelangelo picked himself up. 'Now at exactly what point did we start to lose the upper hand?' he panted.

Donatello fingered a lump on his head. 'Maybe somebody ought to tell him that *we're* the good guys . . .' he said, dazed.

Raphael leaned against a chimney stack to get his breath back. 'Any thoughts?' he said to Leonardo.

'I've only got one thought right now . . .' said Leonardo, staring at the Shredder. 'This guy knows where Master Splinter is.'

The other Turtles nodded with grim determination. Galvanized by concern for their *sensei*, they launched themselves into the fray with renewed fervour. This time even the Shredder was not prepared for the cold ferocity of their assault. He was actually forced back, parrying rapidly with the shaft of the bo. He had never fought such skilful opponents. At last he was able to repel their combined attack — but not before Leonardo's sword had slashed his shoulder. Blood ran through the rent in his *dogi*.

'Where's Splinter?' said Raphael, quietly threatening.

The Shredder glared at the wound. The Turtles' grim resolve had robbed him of his initial advantage. Now he was encircled by four powerful opponents who knew they could hurt him. But the Shredder knew that simple fighting skill was the least part of a ninja's arsenal. Raw cunning was much more important.

'Splinter?' he replied. 'Ah, you mean the rat. So it has a name.' He allowed a split-second to pass before adding with chilling venom: 'It *had* a name.'

'You're lying!' cried Leonardo.

The Shredder snorted in sadistic amusement. 'Am I?'

His taunts had the desired effect. Leonardo forgot his training and flew at him in a rage. The others had no time to step in. The Shredder dropped and kicked at Leonardo's legs, sweeping him over, then jumped up and disarmed him with a slash of the bo. He advanced to plant his foot on the fallen Turtle's chest.

179

The others started forward. The Shredder positioned the point of his weapon over Leonardo's throat. 'Any closer and he dies,' he warned.

The Turtles backed off. They could tell from the Shredder's voice that he would not have the slightest hesitation in killing their brother. He watched them back away with satisfaction, then glanced to the edge of the roof. 'Throw your weapons down – *now*!' he commanded.

They had no choice. Believing that it was the only way to save Leonardo, they tossed their weapons down to the street below.

The Shredder stared at them, the staff-point still pricking Leonardo's throat. 'Fools,' he said derisively. 'The three of you might have overpowered me with only a single fatality.' He gazed down at the helpless Leonardo and raised the weapon for a killing thrust. 'Now you will all share the same fate.'

'No . . !' wailed Raphael forlornly, raising a hand as if to somehow will the weapon immobile.

'Saki.' A cool, clear voice rang out across the rooftop.

The Shredder froze and turned. It was Splinter.

26

The Turtles were overjoyed. They had feared they might never see their beloved teacher again.

With the Shredder distracted, Leonardo rolled away and rejoined the others. They watched Splinter face off against the Shredder. He had a pair of nunchukus tucked into his belt, but he seemed in no hurry to draw it. He appeared almost unconcerned by the Shredder's sharp weapon which was now levelled at his chest.

Michaelangelo took a step forward. He wanted to warn Splinter that this armoured foe was very dangerous. And he was worried that the aged rat was in no condition to fight. 'Master . . .' he began.

Leonardo put out a restraining arm to hold him back. They had all heard Splinter speak of Oroku Saki and the evil deeds he had performed. Now they could see that their master's entire being was focused on just one thing: the Shredder. The connection was obvious. Almost in awe of the tension crackling invisibly between the two old rivals, they slowly backed away to leave an open space between them.

'Yes, Oroku Saki,' said Splinter, 'I know who you are. We met many years ago in the home of my master, Yoshi Hamato.'

Behind the slit of his visor, the Shredder's eyes narrowed as he peered at the rat. Suddenly the truth dawned on him, incredible though it seemed. 'You . . .' he hissed. Reaching up, he detached the faceplate of his helmet. Long disfiguring scars were revealed, the legacy of when Splinter had leapt to attack him on the night of Yoshi's murder.

The Shredder fingered his scars and gave Splinter a scowl full of hatred. 'Now I will finish you, mutant, as I should have done many years ago . . .' A growl welled up from deep in his throat. It sounded like the sound that an enraged wild animal might make when at bay. His face contorting in malevolent fury, he suddenly released his bloodlust in a tremendous battle-cry as he launched himself at Splinter.

Splinter made no move to draw the nunchukus from his belt. He did not even tense up. Instead he almost seemed to relax his posture.

The bo-point shot towards him. It looked to the Turtles as though their master had left himself wide open for the blow, and the Shredder began a triumphant laugh as he bore down on his waiting adversary . . .

Suddenly, in a flash of motion too fast for the eye to follow, Splinter drew the nunchuku sticks and snapped them so that the chain wrapped around the Shredder's bo. At the same moment he leaned aside, angling the nunchukus slightly so that his attacker's momentum was diverted away towards the edge of the roof.

The Shredder's laugh turned to a cry of alarm. It was too late for him to stop. He fell out over the side of the roof, still clinging to the end of his weapon, and frantically seeking to gain a purchase with his toes.

As the lightning-swift instant of action passed, the Shredder was left hanging out into empty space with his feet just braced on the very edge of the roof. The only thing keeping him aloft was his grasp on the bo, the other end of which was wedged between the handles of the nunchukus in Splinter's hand.

Splinter looked down at him almost pityingly. 'Death comes for us all, Oroku Saki,' he said. 'But something much worse comes for you.'

The Shredder struggled grimly to hang on, but he was unable to pull himself up. His lips were drawn back in an expression of insane hatred. He was at Splinter's mercy, but there was no trace of fear on his face. He hardly realized his precarious situation. He only knew that he had to kill his foe

183

at all costs. Taking one hand from the staff, he reached around to a concealed sheath sewn into the lining of his *dogi* and drew out a shuriken.

Splinter saw the shuriken blade flash in the pre-dawn light, but he showed no concern. 'For when *you* die, it will be . . .'

The Shredder's arm shot forward and the shuriken flew straight at Splinter's head. With uncanny ease, the rat reached up and caught it out of the air – releasing his grip on the nunchukus in the process.

For a single instant, the Shredder had time to realize that it was his own unrelenting desire for victory that had sealed his fate. He plummeted with a scream to the ground below, plunging into the rubbish inside Casey's garbage truck.

'. . . without honour,' finished Splinter, staring down.

As the Shredder struggled to get free, Casey flipped a lever. The metallic jaws of the truck closed over the ninja lord. There was a protesting screech as they ground down on his armour. The truck lurched under the unaccustomed strain. Then the jaws clamped shut. The Shredder was gone for ever.

Splinter dropped the shuriken down to join its owner amidst the chewed-up rubbish. At last, after so many years, he had avenged the death of his master. He could finally close the book on that chapter of his past.

As the Turtles rushed forward to embrace their

master, a fleet of police cars came racing belatedly down the street. As they screeched to a halt, the policemen could hardly believe their eyes. The place looked like a war zone, with a broken fire escape twisted across the road and unconscious bodies lying everywhere.

A Channel Three news van was on the scene minutes later. Charles Pennington bundled out. In the distance he could see his son. Danny saw him, too, and ran over towards him. In his rush, he passed April – but he suddenly remembered that there was something important that he had to do. Reaching into his pocket, he pulled out some money, counted out a specific number of notes, and ran back to April.

'April?' He pressed the money into her hand. 'It's something I owe you,' he said. 'Trust me!' Then he turned and, leaving the confused April, ran into his father's arms. 'Dad!' he cried.

Charles was overcome with shock. 'Danny . . .' he said, hugging the boy tightly. 'Danny, Danny, Danny – God, where have you been? I've had the whole city looking for you. Are you OK? Are you all right? Danny?'

Danny grinned and tried to calm his father down. 'It's OK, Dad, I'm fine. Really, I'm fine. And, Dad . . . it's just "Dan" now, OK?'

Charles looked at his son, then hugged him so he wouldn't notice the tears of joy welling up in his eyes. 'Dan . . .'

Then Charles spotted April walking away from

the gathering crowd. She looked dirty and more dishevelled than he had ever seen her. Obviously she was caught up in whatever had happened that night. Charles's eyes lit up and he hurried after her; he scented the chance of a scoop.

April listened to him with a haughty toss of her head. 'If you recall, Charles, I was fired,' she said.

'But, April, there were special circumstances,' pleaded Charles. 'I *need* you to cover this!'

April did not break stride. 'Well, I don't know, Charles. May Williams over at Channel Five has her own office . . .'

'You can have an office.'

April smiled. 'She has a corner office.'

'A corner office, OK,' agreed Charles, nodding urgently. 'Just do the broadcast!'

'She's also the highest paid field reporter in New York.'

Charles winced. April had him over a barrel and she knew it. 'Now you're the highest paid . . .' he conceded.

Beaming broadly, April turned and shook his hand. 'You're a tough negotiator, Charles, but you talked me round. I'll come back.'

The television crew applauded as Charles wiped the beads of nervous sweat from his brow. With the flurry of activity going on all around them, there was no time to lose. He took April's arm and steered her back towards the broadcast van. 'OK, let's get her cleaned up!' he shouted to the crew. 'Somebody throw a blazer on her. Let's go, let's go!'

Another police car drew up and disgorged the heavy bulk of Chief Sterns. He shook his head in bafflement at the scene of mayhem, then immediately began barking orders to the men rounding up the dazed Foot warriors. As the makeup team cleaned her up, April kept her eyes on Sterns with a triumphant smile playing on her lips. She was really going to enjoy interviewing him about this – especially when she got him to admit on air all the mistakes he had made.

Casey came pushing out of the crowd. He almost walked straight past April – she looked so different after a couple of minutes with the makeup team. 'I've been lookin' all over for you,' he said. There was an unusual edge of concern in his voice.

April glanced up. 'Oh, Casey, hi.'

Casey looked himself over. '"Hi"?' he repeated. 'That's *it*? I stand here lookin' like I've just gone two rounds with Mike Tyson and you say "hi"?'

'*Nobody* goes two rounds with Mike Tyson,' said April casually. 'Anyway, you don't need an ambulance, do you?'

Casey stood there. He felt like a big, confused jerk. 'Well, no, but . . .'

April looked up and gave him a warm smile. 'Then just shut up and kiss me, will you? I've got a report to do.'

Casey was taken aback for all of a split-second.

187

Then he stepped forward and swept her into his arms. 'You know,' he said grinning, 'I just love it when you're pushy.'

On the roof, the Turtles and their master were surveying the scene below. They were just as delighted as Casey.

'Woooo . . .!' exclaimed Donatello, rating the kiss. 'Nine point nine five!'

Raphael peered over. 'All right, April!'

'All right, *Casey*!' added Michaelangelo.

Leonardo stood back towards the centre of the roof, beside Splinter. He looked to where a line of daylight was breaking in the east, outlining the city in red gold. Filled with exhilaration, he pumped his fist into the air. 'Weren't we awesome?' he cried out of sheer exuberance.

'Bodacious!' said Michaelangelo.

'Excellent!' said Raphael.

'Fabuloso!' said Donatello.

They fell silent as Splinter raised a finger. No doubt he would offer them a wise Zen saying that would help them learn from the events of that night . . .

'I have always liked . . . "cowabunga",' remarked Splinter.

The Turtles just stared at him for a moment, amazed. Then, as huge grins spread across their faces, they punched the air in unison and gave their new battlecry: 'Cowa-*bun*-ga!'

Splinter watched them with an indulgent smile. They were more than his pupils – they were his adopted sons. Their youthful high spirits gave pleasure to the weary old rat. And in fact, he had an old Zen expression that fitted the occasion perfectly:

Sitting still and looking wise does not compare to having a good time and making lots of noise.

Whoever said that could almost have had the Turtles in mind!

THE END